Why Stuff Matters

Why Stuff Matters

JEN WALDO

A

Arcadia Books Ltd
139 Highlever Road
London W10 6PH

www.arcadiabooks.co.uk

First published in the United Kingdom 2017

A catalogue record for this book is available from the British Library.

ISBN 978-1-911350-22-4

Typeset in Garamond by MacGuru Ltd
Printed and bound by TJ International, Padstow PL28 8RW

ARCADIA BOOKS DISTRIBUTORS ARE AS FOLLOWS:

in the UK and elsewhere in Europe:
BookSource
50 Cambuslang Road
Cambuslang
Glasgow G32 8NB

in Australia/New Zealand:
NewSouth Books
University of New South Wales
Sydney NSW 2052

Why Stuff Matters

In memory of my mother
Beatrice Crawford Haenisch Peery
1935–2016

The Tornado

My antique mall is the only building in this part of town that has a basement, so as soon as our county is included in the tornado warning that streams across the bottom of the television screen, I tromp down to the main floor from my third-floor living quarters, unlock the front door, and prepare to be overrun for the fourth time this month.

Stepping out to the sidewalk, I peer at the night sky. The clouds are churning. Out on Paramount Boulevard the traffic lights bob and sway. Usually tornado warnings don't amount to much, but it looks like a storm's definitely heading our way.

People from the apartments across the street lean into the wind as they make their way to the shelter I'm offering. The low-cost housing is mostly inhabited by Latinos with lots of kids. I bet they have as many as ten people per unit over there. I recognize a few faces, but I don't know names. They keep to themselves.

Beyond the apartments, bordered by a tall wooden fence, is a residential area. The houses back there are old, and the people who live in them are also old; and, for the most part, these elderly people feel disdainful toward the stocky figures who live in the apartments and don't speak much English. But their homes also lack storm shelters, so many of them, too, will come.

< 1 >

Excited by the change in routine, the kids'll become wild when they get inside. As the caretaker of this cavernous building full of other people's stuff, this is the inevitability that I am expected to address. The apartment crowd shuffles and bounces its way inside and presses toward the central staircase. Watching for stragglers, I herd them down to the basement, leaving the door unlocked.

I allow these people inside because it's the right thing to do, and because it's what my mother did. Mom was always concerned for the welfare of others; and that apartment building is no more substantial than a cracker box. But shouldn't they reciprocate by reining in their offspring? The children have been here often enough to know their favorite points of interest. The kids' section is in the back of the basement and, with noisy enthusiasm, they skip and run and hop in that direction. I head them off, making sweeping motions with my arms spread wide, shooing them back to their parents, who huddle around the bottom of the stairs. A sloppy group, they chat with one another and make no attempt to control their children. Within me a small flame of temper ignites. This is a place of business, not an amusement park.

The stooped people from the houses arrive. Nervously clutching the handrails to steady their descent, they're weighted with heavy coats, purses, and small bits of luggage. A gaunt and gray crowd, they cringe as they encounter the children's strident energy.

The kids make a game of eluding me. They run between the bins of carefully organized comic books, past shelves of action figures still in their original boxes, around display cases full of superhero memorabilia. Ken, the owner of the booth, would shudder to see his territory invaded in this way.

< 2 >

Over in the toy booth a fat four-year-old girl bounces on Estelle's most prized item, an eighty-year-old mint-condition rocking horse. A sign is posted in front of the horse – Do Not Ride Unless You Want to Buy. It's priced at eighteen hundred dollars. If anything happens to that horse Estelle will be crushed by grief.

Movement on the stairs catches my eye and I'm relieved to see Marlina (long i) and Carly marching downward, two hefty seventy-somethings on a mission. They both have booths on the second floor – Marlina sells china and crystal; Carly sells jewelry, both costume and fine. These two live closer than any of the other vendors, which is why they were able to come in and help me keep an eye on things.

Marlina's rosy-cheeked countenance grows furious when she catches sight of the girl on the horse.

'Hey you! Get off there right now!' she shouts, waving her arms as her agitation impels her forward. She glares at the crowd of parents. 'Parents, control your children or out you go!'

They look at her like she's making no sense. No one claims the girl who has changed from bouncing up and down to lunging forward and back. Good God, she's working up a sweat. Marlina's a force and she doesn't like to be disregarded. She steps forward, reaches out, ready to grab the girl by the arm and yank her off.

'No, Marlina!' I leap in front of her, blocking her way. 'Are you looking to get sued?'

'Estelle would die if she saw how that girl's abusing that horse.'

'Do you think everybody's in?' I ask. 'I'm going to check the building.'

Upstairs, I take a walk through the first and second floors,

< 3 >

peering carefully into dark corners and listening for sneaky movements. Last time we were taken over this way a couple of small items disappeared – a Wedgwood candy dish and a pair of opera glasses. Of course the vendors blamed me. But what am I supposed to do, turn these people away? I promised to be more vigilant next time, and I instigated a policy stating that, during tornado season, owners must secure their more valuable pieces behind lock and key before going home – and that really got folks riled because they've been doing things the same way for thirty years and who am I to come in and make changes?

Back on the first floor, I look out through the storefront glass and, in the reflection, see myself – a tall blond woman looking anxious. Beyond my image, I can't see anyone else heading this way, but I decide to leave the door unlocked just in case. Some of the people from the neighborhood drove their cars over instead of walking. I don't like that a dozen cars are parked right in front of my broad window, a hazard. The sky is an eerie shade of pinkish gray, lending an odd light to the street and buildings.

And then I witness the birth of the tornado. About four football fields in front of where I'm standing, on the other side of the apartments, a funnel pokes from beneath the skirt of the clouds. Within seconds it's a live beast reaching for earth. It writhes and stirs until it makes touchdown.

Part of a roof is lifted up. Debris spins and is flung in all directions.

The noise is fearsome, the rumbling of a thousand jet engines. And explosions add to the mayhem – pops, bangs, bams, and pows. A particularly loud *Boom!* is followed by the lights going out. A frightened moan rises from the basement as the building is plunged into darkness.

And then the long planks marking the boundary between

< 4 >

the apartments and the neighborhood are plucked up, one-by-one, as though there's order behind this chaos.

The mighty tempest tears right through the apartment building. Walls burst apart. Scraps of drywall and bits of furniture fly upward and disappear. The awning over the cars in the apartment parking lot is torn away and hurled; then the cars and trucks are pushed, lifted, and flipped. A wooden door crashes on to the roof of a Buick in front of the building. A couple of car alarms go off.

And I hover here, mesmerized by this glorious destruction, as though the storefront glass is a protective shield. What an idiot.

The twister veers left down Paramount Boulevard, taking out every building, sign, light pole, and car on the other side, leaving my property untouched.

< 5 >

Pard's Death

In the morning rescue workers with dogs come and search the remains of the apartment building. Three bodies are excavated, along with a five-year-old boy, still alive, who is taken to the hospital. News crews park their vans in front of my building. For the whole day pictures of the rubble across the street, along with photos of the three men who died there, are shown on the cable news stations. Where once there was an apartment building, now there's a ragged jumble of couches at odd angles, upside-down washing machines, and cars and trucks crushed by slabs of concrete. The houses on the other side of the apartment didn't fare too badly – only one home lost its roof, but the rest were left intact.

If there's one thing I know about tornadoes it's that they're capricious. This one skipped all over town, kicking up and down like a chorus girl. It took out the education building of the Lutheran church, but respectfully left the sanctuary alone. It wiped out the Sears store, cutting it off at the entrance to the mall with impressive precision; power tools, still in their packaging, were scattered all over the place. It took out the new elementary school which was the only school in town with a storm shelter; and though this was discussed on the local news as a pertinent aspect, the shelter really didn't matter because not only had school

< 6 >

already let out for the summer, the tornado swooped through on a Sunday night when no one would have been there anyway.

More relevant in my small sphere is that one of our own was killed. Pard Kemp – Pard being a nickname derived from a nickname. Eighty-six years old. It looks like his decision to take shelter in the basement of the Baptist church came thirty seconds too late; he was knocked on the head by a flying brick in the parking lot. He was an offensive old guy – smelly, the way some old people get when they're too tired to shower or do laundry. He had very little hair, only a few teeth, and an ornery disposition that made everybody wish he'd just go somewhere and die, which he finally did.

Pard operated the double-sized booth at the rear of the second floor, as far from the front door as possible. Secretive by nature, he preferred an inconvenient location. His is one of the more enticing booths – small household implements from the last half of the eighteen hundreds. Irons, washboards, chamber pots, bellows, cuspidors, farm tools. Wandering through his booth is like a trip back in time, and who doesn't enjoy that?

Most troublesome is what he kept out of sight, locked in the deep bottom drawer of the cabinet at the back of his booth – handguns. The guns were most likely slipped from sweaty palm to sweaty palm, offered in payment for sly favors, or given to Pard for safekeeping. Unfettered by banalities such as documentation or licensing, the question about what to do with them is going to get the vendors worked up.

I checked earlier; there are a dozen of the bothersome things. I know nothing about small firearms. Most are black or dark gray; a couple of them are silver; some are smooth; some have textured grips. Manufacturers' names are etched

< 7 >

on the barrel or grip – Filigree, Walther, Desert Eagle, and Beretta. Various sizes, different barrel lengths. Mostly pistols, only two revolvers. Ammunition is boxed and set to the side – cartridges and bullets in different sizes. I have no idea what cartridges correspond to what weapons. It surprises me that they have an odor – machine oil is my guess.

Pard had no living family and he left no will. While this means his modest house on the west side will go to the state, the state's not going to step in and claim all his old fixtures, tools, and prairie paraphernalia. I've scheduled a meeting to discuss the allocation of his inventory.

Around noon I haul the plastic chairs from the storage area in the east corner and set them up at the T-junction right in front of his booth. The vendors begin to limp in. There are forty-five of them, and all are in attendance, except Janet, who's in Fort Worth awaiting the birth of her first great-grandchild. When everybody's found a seat, I take the center position at the entrance to the booth. The folks shift and glare at each other and me. They're grumpy. Every one of them is certain they're going to lose out or be taken advantage of in some way.

'I should just absorb it all.' Dee's laying claim right from the start. 'It'll fit right in with my inventory.'

I'm glad to see Dee's sharp side; she's been vague lately, forgetting names and getting turned around in the building. Her assertion is reasonable. Though her space is themed around a more feminine motif – brush-and-comb sets, jewelry boxes, elegant shawls and gloves of lace – her stock is from the same era. But of course this solution isn't acceptable to the others.

'You've got no right to any of it,' Will says. 'I've known Pard for fifty years.' Technically true, though they were hardly fond of one another.

< 8 >

'I get the guns.' This from Sherman, who thinks that seeing action in Korea entitles him to the weaponry. His inventory is military gear – service medals, canteens, hats and helmets, belts and boots. I guess he thinks small arms will fit in nicely.

'No,' I say. 'They've got no documentation. I'm turning them over to the police.'

As proprietor of this raggedy-ass business, it's my job to at least keep things looking like they're on the up-and-up. My announcement is met with grumbling, which is nothing new. I haven't done a thing since I took over last year that hasn't been met with grumbling.

The reason for their objection isn't that I've made an unfair or unwise decision. The problem is that these obsessive old people can't bear to watch anything walk out the door. Handing the guns to the police goes against their code. Here, in this place, you don't give things away. Every item has a price and until that price is met the item doesn't move. Their attachment to their stuff is evident in the way they overprice every item (eighteen hundred dollars for a *toy*), the way they always manage to be elsewhere when someone who sincerely wants to buy walks through, the way they down-talk some of their best items.

'What if we can unload them for a decent price?' Carly asks.

'That's what we'll do.' Will's taking over. 'We sell them and split the money.'

'Or one of us keeps them and buys everybody else out,' Sherman says.

'I'll allow them to remain on the premises for two weeks.' I'm becoming adept at compromise. Dealing with these folks requires constant give-and-take. 'If no one's come up with a buyer by then, I'll have no choice but to call the cops

< 9 >

to come get them. If a single buyer among you wants all of them, I'm making the stipulation that they're moved off the property.'

I don't care where they go; I just want them gone. It's not like any among us is going to take a moral stance. At least half this group is involved in some form of legal misconduct.

Barry, whose booth holds jukeboxes and turntables from the sixties, buys electronics from pasty-faced men who slink in and out during off-hours. These items are never put on display; he furtively sells them from his back storage area. And Carly does the same, only with jewelry.

Roxy Lynn basically runs an unlicensed pawnshop, dealing primarily in musical instruments.

And Sue. Every member of her extended family has a doctor or two writing prescriptions for pills they don't need, and they route them through her. There's a constant stream of all kinds of people between the front door and her booth.

I doubt there's a single one of these vendors who isn't running one kind of scam or another. And the few of us who aren't actually cavorting on the dark side are silently complicit.

'Two weeks,' I repeat. 'Then I'm turning them over to the authorities.'

Whatever side schemes Pard had going were lucrative. He's been storing his cash in the safe in Mom's office – my office, now – for years, as do several others. Up until this morning I had no idea how much money was in his box.

Thirty-seven thousand.

In my safe.

My safe.

Mine.

< 10 >

The Safe

The safe is quite large, practically the size of a panic room. It's almost as tall as I am and twice as broad. The combination lock opens to my birthday, which was sweet of Mom. The interior consists of a central open area with shelves adjusted to different heights on three sides. Most of the vendors have small lockboxes tucked beneath their counters, but Mom didn't mind providing this safe in the office for those who felt like they needed a more secure storage space. Her method of organization involved metal padlocked containers the size of boot boxes labeled with the name of the owner. The box owners were each given a key, and she had possession of the spare keys, which was reasonable as it was her safe. She promised she would never go into their boxes without profound cause, and the people who used the safe trusted her. She was the only one with the combination to the safe itself – and now that honor belongs to me. I'm just coming to realize what Mom knew all along – that these folks squirrel away massive amounts of cash and then they die. There are fourteen padlocked boxes in there. Do they all hold as much money as Pard's?

I haven't really taken time to think about this before, but now I'm wondering what's going through the minds of these people I deal with daily. During their middle years every one of them held regular jobs, raised kids, owned

< 11 >

homes, sensibly kept their money in banks, and paid taxes. Then their kids moved away and the jobs, too, fell away, and the social security they paid into for all those years was enough to keep them fed but not enough to pay for a new roof or to buy a new car when the old one fell apart.

So I guess they thought – why don't I make some money by selling all the old stuff I've collected through the years? And hey, if I don't declare it or keep it in a bank, nobody'll know I have it. Then, in predictable reaction to their own dishonest dealings, paranoia crept in. Every last one of them is certain that everybody's after everything they've got. They're suspicious and cagey and constantly vigilant; and this distrust has worn them down until they're cantankerous and stubborn.

These are the concepts I'm pondering when the desk phone rings.

'Caprock Antiques and Gifts,' I answer.

'Is this Jessica Hockley?' Businesslike tone, woman.

'Yes.'

'I'm calling from the Caprock and Tri-county Morgue about Pard Kemp.'

'What can I do for you?'

'He had you down as his emergency contact.'

'Oh good God.' I wonder how many others have me down as their emergency contact. The majority of them, I bet. 'He didn't have any family.'

'Yes, it's my understanding that he was alone. Ordinarily in this circumstance we simply cremate. Is that okay with you?'

'Sure.'

'As his friend, would you like to claim his ashes?'

Besides the vendors' boxes, the safe holds three urns. I think about them now. And then I think about Pard, a

< 12 >

grasping old man, keeping company with my loved ones. His remains don't belong in my care.

'No,' I tell her. 'I suppose you have a protocol for this situation.'

'Yes. We'll see to it.'

'Thanks,' I say before ending the call.

I imagine a massive storage facility for unclaimed ashes. Of the forty-five vendors, only ten of them have family members who care for them. The rest, like Pard, are alone. How many times, in the years to come, will I be receiving this same call?

There's a knock on the door. I look up.

'Hey, Roxy Lynn,' I say.

Roxy's a tiny woman with the rough complexion that comes from smoking for seventy years. Her hair is an unlikely shade of pink and she always does her nails in bright red. Taking pride in being tidy, she's the sort who irons her jeans, tucks in her shirts, and accessorizes carefully. As mentioned earlier, she runs an unlicensed pawnshop, dealing in trumpets, flutes, and guitars – but occasionally a bicycle or Rolex will appear in her area.

She slides inside, closing the door behind her like she's going to share a big secret.

'I need to borrow one of Pard's guns.' Her poorly fitted bridge gives her a slight lisp. 'Raymond's back in town.'

Raymond is her ex-husband and his being back in town is nothing new. He lives in Las Vegas, but every so often he shows up in Caprock. And while he's here he goes out to Roxy's, hollers obscenities through the locked screen door, and perpetrates some annoying vandalism like uprooting her mailbox or throwing a rock through a window. Then he goes away. I can't imagine what his expectations are – the two of them have been divorced for thirty years.

< 13 >

'You've never needed to borrow one before.'

Her little house is five miles north of Caprock on FM 92, set far back on a large country lot, at least two miles away from the nearest neighbor. Living out there, the question isn't why she needs to borrow a gun as much as it's why doesn't she already have one.

'You think you know things you just don't know. Pard loaned me the Beretta every time Raymond came to town.'

'He let you check out a gun like it was a library book?'

'Exactly.'

'How much did he charge?'

'Nothing. Pard was helpful. He cared about my safety.'

She's lying. It wasn't in Pard's nature to do a favor without money changing hands. Her deifying him is typical. Pretty soon everyone in the building's going to be rhapsodizing about what a saint he was. They remember others the way they want to be remembered.

'I just don't believe that. How long do you think you'll need it?'

'A week, maybe ten days.'

'Two hundred bucks a week.'

'Pard only charged one-fifty.'

'Take it or leave it.'

She tightens her jaw, glares resentfully and, with a huff, stomps from the office.

My phone starts vibrating. Caller ID signals Joe Epps, a guy I knew in high school. Joe's trying to get something going with me for no other reason than he got divorced and I moved back to town. Though I'll admit, the few times we went out when we were younger, we did make a pretty couple – him tall and dark, me tall and golden, both of us athletic and clear-skinned. These days I have no interest in dating and no concern at all over what I see when I look in

< 14 >

the mirror. I let it go to voice mail. I wish he'd stop calling. The last thing I need is a detective with the Caprock PD coming anywhere near this warren of petty criminals.

A few minutes later Roxy returns, and she's brought backup. Will and Sherman, two tough negotiators, follow her in and close the door. I don't like this one bit.

'You're ganging up on me?'

'You want to charge Roxy two hundred a week,' Will says. 'What I want to know is, what're you going to do with that money, and who says you have a right to it? And why do you think you're the one should be making decisions about those guns?'

'Those guns've been stored and left behind in my building. I'm willing to work with you folks, but ultimately, what happens with them is my call.' I claim ownership of this building like it's impressive, but we all know that the electricity and plumbing need complete overhauls, the dingy walls need paint, and the handrails on the stairs are too wobbly to be safe. There's no denying that Caprock Antiques and Gifts, left to me by my mother, needs money spent on maintenance. I'll get to it eventually. These days, though, I have no impetus. I'm a ditherer.

'She could buy a gun for what you're charging,' Will tells me.

'Then why doesn't she?'

They shift uncomfortably, not wanting to acknowledge what we all know: Roxy's got a past that includes a stint in prison. It's a titillating story, whispered into the ear of all newcomers, about how she and her first husband, Vance Arckle, had a volatile relationship, throwing objects and accusations at each other, screaming until the police were called; until, in her fury, she plowed Vance down with his own truck. Though it happened back in the seventies, the

< 15 >

authorities don't pass out guns to someone who's taken a life.

'When someone dies, unless they've said otherwise, their property is split among us,' Sherman says. Bald, with heavy lenses in his glasses, he looks a lot nicer than he is. 'That's fair and it's the way we've always done it. It's the way Alicia wanted it done.' I hate it when they use my mother on me.

'Why don't we put any money derived from the guns – rented or sold – into a fund to pay for the Christmas party?'

Last year's party was lame and they blamed me. In my defense, I thought it was a chip-in event where everybody donated a few dollars and I took the money and bought snacks at the grocery store. But apparently I was supposed to hire SBBQ (Southern Barbecue) to cater. I later looked into it and SBBQ would have charged seven hundred. The collection brought in two hundred. Apparently my mother made up the difference for years and, in the spirit of Secret Santa, never said a word. So how was I to know?

'No, ma'am,' Will says. 'We pay for the Christmas party ourselves, just like we always have.'

They have no idea.

'Then how about using the money to pay for a new security system?'

I've been worried about this ever since I moved in here. I live in this monstrosity all by myself and the outdated security system only covers the commercial floors. The top floor, my floor, has no alarm system at all. Sometimes I get scared at night. Also, an issue yet to be addressed is that several of these people have their own key to the building. They know the security code. They won't want me changing the current system.

'That's your responsibility. You're supposed to see to the building. That's why we pay rent.'

< 16 >

'What is it you're wanting me to do here, Will?'

'Any money derived from the guns is split among us.'

'You want me to split two hundred dollars forty-five ways?' Forty-five people behind a gun-renting operation, definitely one of the most outlandish schemes I've participated in. But hey, it's a negotiation, so I say, 'I get a double cut because I'm handling the logistics and, ultimately, I'm the responsible party.'

'Done.'

Then I spend a couple of hours going to the bank and turning the four fifties Roxy gave me into small bills and change so that I can distribute four dollars and twenty-three cents to every vendor in the building. And I take for myself eight dollars and fifty-one cents.

< 17 >

Normal Behavior

At seven I turn out the light in the office and go to the front to lock the door. The news vans have moved on and across the street the bulldozers have been busy. The rubble from the apartment building has been pushed into a gigantic heap of cement and broken walls and planks. Furniture, toys, cars, and appliances are in there, too. In memory of the three who died, people have been bringing flowers and placing them on a cleared space of the sidewalk. It's the hottest time of year. By morning the well-intended flowers will just mean more mess to clean up.

I head toward the back exit, to the rear lot where most of us park our cars – the few who have booths toward the front of the building prefer to park in the front lot. As usual, I'm going to the grocery store to get something for dinner. I maintain a stark lifestyle in my spacious loft (an upmarket term for the top floor of this rundown building). I have no washer and dryer; I do my laundry at the laundromat. My air conditioner is a window unit, and I have only a single electric burner and no refrigerator. My usual evening fare is a salad composed at the grocery store salad bar and a patty or fish portion fried in a warped pan on the cooking ring.

When I come out of the building, Joe is leaning against the dented fender of a maroon Impala. He straightens when he sees me approaching.

< 18 >

'Go to dinner with me,' he says, adding, 'please?'

With dark brown curly hair, striking blue eyes, and a charming crooked smile, he's a fine-looking guy, though he's put on a little weight since high school, and when he drops the smile his lips slip easily into a scowl.

'That's the ugliest vehicle I've ever seen.'

'Department issue.'

And oh good God, he's holding out a wrapped bouquet of yellow roses. I cannot help myself: I roll my eyes. Either he's attempting to manipulate or he's got romantic aspirations. I have no patience with either. And while I'd like to be someone who's careful with the feelings of others, sometimes it's best just to dole out the unpleasant truth.

'I figure you come with a thousand bucks a month in child support,' I tell him, 'and rumor has it that the reason for your split with Kim is that you cheated. If it weren't for a department car you'd have no car at all. But hey, lots of women appreciate a good-looking man with clean fingernails – only you're going to have to find someone who's way more desperate than I am.'

'Calling it like you see it, just like old times.' You'd think my harsh words would give him pause, but not so. Still offering the flowers, he straightens from the car and takes a step toward me. 'It's just dinner. Wouldn't you like to sit across the table from someone and have a meal and conversation? It's what normal people do.'

What normal people do. The grief counselor I was seeing in Dayton said that, with time, pretending would become reality. Do I have it in me to pretend to be normal? It's a possibility I should probably explore.

'Let me run upstairs and comb my hair,' I tell him.

I snatch the flowers and hurry up the outside staircase without asking him in. I stick the roses in an oversized

< 19 >

glass; they make a cheerful display on my kitchen table. I pass a comb through my dull blonde hair, spray it out of my eyes, and change one T-shirt for another.

Half an hour later we're sharing chips and salsa at Manuela's Cocina.

'So, I heard Pard Kemp died,' he says with a speculative squint.

'Yeah.'

'Quite a gun collection he had.'

'Really? Not that I know of.' I've made a promise to the vendors. I'm pretty sure I manage to look genuinely befuddled, an expression that's always come naturally to me.

'Come on, Jess. Everybody in town knew about it.'

'Everybody in town was wrong.'

'Pard was into all kinds of things. Rumor has it that at one time he sheltered illegals on their way up north – for a price. Also, I heard he was behind the airport restaurant scam back in the eighties, when they sold those out-of-date hotdogs that made so many people sick.'

I don't know anything about bad hotdogs, but it's just the kind of thing Pard would've been involved in.

'Sounds like you've listened to lots of gossip about stuff that happened a long time ago.' In this aspect, Joe hasn't changed. He still believes that all it takes to make something true is to say it out loud.

'So you haven't come across any handguns of questionable origin?'

'Absolutely not. But hey, check out his house. He lived there for his whole adult life, so chances are there's a gun or two lying around.'

The mention of this reminds me of something the vendors seem to have forgotten. The stuff in Pard's house.

< 20 >

It's not like them to leave a man's personal possessions to the state without picking through them first.

'Already did. No guns.'

'We'll be clearing out his booth in a day or two. If we come across anything that doesn't look right, I'll let you know, even though I'm sure you're wrong on this one.'

'I tell you what – why don't I come have a look-see?'

'You don't believe me?'

'Sure I believe you. But what kind of cop would I be if I didn't verify it for the record? So I'll stop by tomorrow and see what's what.'

'I'm busy tomorrow.' He can't poke around in that booth without my permission.

'Day after, then.'

Which gives me a day to find someplace else to stash them.

'I heard you were married,' he says.

'Was. Not anymore.'

'Yeah, divorce is the worst.' It's natural that he'd assume divorce. It's easier to take than the truth, so I let it stand.

'Tell me about being a cop,' I say, hoping he'll tell me about his life instead of trying to find out about mine. And it works. For the rest of the meal he talks about his training, the time he spent in uniform, department politics, and the hoops he had to jump through to make detective.

He returns me to the back of my building at nine-thirty. There's an awkward moment when he leans in, lips-first, for a kiss, and I give him my cheek. He pulls back, surprised that I'm not receptive.

'It's not going to happen,' I tell him. 'Thanks for dinner.'

'Can't blame a guy for trying.'

He waits in the car as I ascend the stairs and unlock my door. When I'm inside I hear him drive off.

< 21 >

How did I handle a normal dinner on a weeknight with a guy I used to know? Did acting normal make me feel normal? No, it just made me feel sad.

A little after midnight my phone rings. Caller ID tells me it's Roxy.

'Roxy Lynn, it's the middle of the night. I'm sleeping.'

'I shot Raymond dead and I need you to get out here and help me.'

'Is this a joke? Are you fooling with me?'

'Right between the eyes, right on my front porch, swear to God.'

'Call the cops.'

'Cops tend to arrest you when you shoot someone.'

'He was threatening you on your property.'

Nobody in the Panhandle would send an eighty-something woman to prison for protecting herself.

'Getting arrested means giving my hard-earned money to a lawyer.'

As always with these people, it comes down to money.

'Also,' she continues, 'there's the matter of the Beretta. The cops'd want to know where I got it.'

'I'm on my way.'

That puny double share wasn't worth the trouble.

< 22 >

Death by Roxy

The route to Roxy's is convoluted, and the roads go down in quality with each turn – the highway, a farm-to-market road, several miles of pitted tarmac, then, for the last half-mile, rough dirt. She lives way out, far from anybody, miles from neighborhoods and shops.

In town the streetlights and headlights dominate, whereas out here the darkness is the prevailing presence. The barbed-wire fence that runs parallel to the road casts angled shadows on the mesquite-dotted landscape. After my eyes grow accustomed I notice the twinkling stars and the bright full moon and the fluffy gray clouds sweeping across the sky.

When I've still got a mile to go, I pull on to the shoulder and get out of the car. I need some time to prepare myself for what I'm going to be dealing with at Roxy's. Circling the hood, I rest my backside on the fender, stare at the flat shadowy landscape, and ask myself the same question I've been asking ever since I moved back to Caprock. What the hell am I doing here?

The crux is that it's impossible to analyze the last year without thinking about what came before. I open the door to my memories, only a tiny crack; but the pain is quick and sharp, like a bite, and I recoil and slam the door.

The rush of the wind fills my ears. The heads of the

< 23 >

stunted Texas shrubs bow toward the east; and the light-hearted clouds in the sky also head that way.

A movement on the ground about ten feet in front of where I stand catches my eye, and I realize that I'm on the edge of a vast and active prairie dog colony. The little guys are popping up and down and scurrying everywhere. Off to the left an owl swoops, grabs, and emits a triumphant 'Whoo!' as it rises.

Okay, introspection over. I get back in the car and drive the final distance.

There's no proper driveway at Roxy's. Everybody who comes out here just pulls up to the clear area in front of the small house. It looks like I'm not the only one she called.

In addition to Roxy's ancient Camry, a Chevy truck, a Malibu, and a beat-up Ford with Nevada plates are parked there. As I turn into an open space my headlights sweep across four people on the porch. They stand in a circle, three gray heads and a pink one turned downward as they stare at some central attraction. It doesn't take much imagination to know what they're looking at.

Right between the eyes, she said, right on the front porch.

And who, besides me, has Roxy Lynn invited to help her deal with her ex-husband's lifeless form?

Sherman, a blowhard who stopped allowing new ideas to penetrate around nineteen-seventy.

Ken, who wears superhero T-shirts and sometimes forgets that the characters of his Marvel memorabilia aren't real.

And Barry, shifty dealer in dubiously obtained electronics.

As I roll to a stop next to Ken's Malibu, they all turn and look my way. The three men look disheveled – shirts not tucked in or hanging crookedly, jowls misted with silver bristles. Roxy, too, looks mussed. Her feathery hair, usually tamed by product, dances and flies in the wind.

< 24 >

'So, what's the plan?' I ask as I get out of the car. I drag my feet, reluctant to join them beneath the porch light. Roxy's been a heavy smoker for years and, though no one is smoking, the smell of cigarettes rides the whipping currents.

'We're gonna dig a grave,' Barry says.

He shifts to the side, a signal for me to join their circle, which I do. I look down at Raymond. The hole in his forehead doesn't look all that lethal – a small blood-filled dot, that's all. It's hard to discern his character from the lines of his slack face. Frown furrows are carved between his eyebrows, right below Roxy's centered bullet hole. Deep creases at the sides of his mouth indicate an anxious nature. I estimate, from his features, that he was well into his eighties. How can a man so old cause so much disruption?

'I got the perfect spot picked out for him,' Roxy says. 'It's just a matter of getting it dug and dropping him in.'

Her property stretches behind the house for a couple of acres. The casual acceptance of her ex-husband's crude grave so close to the place where she eats and sleeps makes me wonder how many other bodies she's got buried back there. Also, the way she has a place picked out for him seems awfully convenient.

'Did you plan this?' I ask, more disturbed by the possibility of being duped than the thought of her planning a murder. 'Did you deliberately set out to kill this man?'

'What? No! Though I won't say I didn't foresee the likelihood. When he showed up belligerent and making demands, I warned him. I pointed the muzzle right at him and told him to get off my property. Only he was too drunk or too stupid to back off. So I did what I had to do.'

'Good thing there's been rain recently,' Sherman says. Ordinarily the dry Texas dirt is packed hard. But the storm that passed through dumped tubs, so the task won't be impossible.

< 25 >

And now I know why she assembled this particular group. Barry and Ken are roommates, so if she calls one, she's calling both. Also, in their seventies, they're the youngest strongest men she knows. And Sherman has the truck that'll transport Raymond to the site. But why am I here?

'Why did you bring me into this?' I ask, indignant at being included in this gruesome escapade.

'You said so yourself – you're the responsible party.'

I did indeed make that claim. Am I responsible for this?

'Are you sure he's dead?' Part of me still thinks this is an elaborate prank.

'I know dead and this is definitely it,' Sherman says. Then, thinking of his truck bed, he asks, 'Got any plastic sheeting?'

'Why sure. I just happen to have some,' Roxy tells him.

Disappearing through the front door she comes out with a package containing painter's tarp. She rips the pack open and she and I, and Barry and Ken, spread the plastic sheet beside Raymond. Then we each take hold of an appendage, lift Raymond's body, and position him at the center of the tarp, swaddling his stiffening corpse and tucking in the corners so he's wrapped like a giant burrito.

Meanwhile Sherman has repositioned his truck and put the back down, so the transfer is only a matter of getting the body down the few stairs and sliding it in. Two shovels are propped next to the door, and Barry sticks them in next to Raymond. Roxy rides around to the back with Sherman, and Ken, Barry, and I follow on foot. The truck stops about sixty yards from the house, adjacent to what was once a fence, but now is just a couple of leaning planks.

At first we all take turns, two at a time, digging the hole – except for Roxy, who's just too arthritic and weak for such activity. But mud is heavy and the men are old and out of shape. After his second stint, Sherman, mid-eighties, turns

< 26 >

a dangerous shade of puce. Then Ken has difficulty catching his breath, and Barry loses all feeling in his hands. The last couple of feet fall to me; and I'm so angry about this whole ugly fiasco that I attack the muddy earth with gusto, taking pleasure in the strain across my back and shoulders, and making a mess of my shoes and the bottom of my jeans. I'm not an efficient gravedigger and what should be a tight deep rectangle ends up being a broad bowl. And there's no way the phrase 'six feet under' applies. Maybe four. We place the tarp-wrapped body in the center and I scoop the mud back in. We tramp over it, packing and smoothing, but when we're done there's still a slight mound; it's obvious that the area has been disturbed.

'What're you going to do with his car?' I ask.

'Charlie'll take care of it.' I have yet to figure out exactly what sneaky activity supplements Charlie's income. From his booth he sells hubcaps and other car accessories. I haven't looked beyond that.

'Do you want to say something to mark the occasion?' Barry asks Roxy Lynn. 'He was your husband at one time.'

'Raymond was a drunk and a cheat. His whole life he never thought of anyone but himself and he never finished anything he set out to do. So I'll just say thanks to all of you for your help. Anything I can do to return the favor, let me know.'

The rising sun peeks through pink clouds, making our shadows long and thin. Every one of us, except Roxy, has thick brown mud caked to mid-calf.

'I've got the Beretta in the house if you want to take it back,' Roxy says.

'You've got it for the rest of the week,' I say, 'just in case there's anybody else who's earned your disfavor.'

To my dismay, though I was being facetious, she decides to hang on to it.

< 27 >

Moving the Stash

Jessica,
I hope hearing from me doesn't dredge up painful memories. I think about you often and I worry about how you're doing. I hope moving back to Caprock was the right decision, and that all is going well for you. When you get a chance, please drop me a line to let me know you're still out there somewhere.
Take care,
Valerie

Valerie was one of my fellow teachers in Dayton, where I taught fourth grade before my husband and baby daughters died. Every once in a while I hear from someone back there. The few years I taught school and was friends with Valerie were happy ones. And then the happiness went away.

I delete the email, push away from the desk, and step out of my office. Being up most of the night has made me achy and slow.

I like this time of day in the building. It's silent and vast, full of shadows and history. The vendors will start coming in to attend to their booths in an hour or so. Not everybody shows up every day so I don't know whose faces I will see, whose complaints I will hear. While we didn't really reach

< 28 >

a definitive conclusion yesterday about what to do with Pard's stuff, I've already noticed the other booths absorbing it.

Kathryn's area is the first one customers see when they walk through the door. Mainly she has a kitchen collection – lovely cup-and-saucer sets, delicate cream pitchers, whimsical cookie jars. And now several of Pard's porcelain kettles and bowls take up a section on the middle shelf along the left side of her area. When they were in his booth they were placed randomly and covered with dust. Kathryn's polished them and arranged them artistically.

Dee, whose collection mainly runs to lace and linens, has placed one of Pard's anvils on the floor propping up a shawl-draped mirror, its position implying use as a doorstop.

And Sue has arranged the three sets of bellows between two McCoy pitchers, which are further framed by two spinning wheels – a stylish tableau of incongruous objects. Typically, she's got the bellows overpriced – two-twenty a set.

Knowing that this same thing will happen with the guns if I don't get them out of Pard's booth, I must move quickly. The reasonable place to store them would be the safe in the office. But it's too public; too many people require regular access. It takes three up-and-down trips to move the firearms and ammunition to my living quarters. Placing them on the kitchen table next to the yellow roses Joe gave me, I sit down and study my surroundings, looking fruitlessly for a serviceable hiding place. With eighteen-foot ceilings and no inner walls, this was never meant to be a dwelling. I only have a few basic pieces of furniture – a table with two chairs, a small couch in front of a television, a plain chest for my clothes, and a bed with a basic frame. The partitions that mark off the bathroom don't reach the ceiling.

< 29 >

The floor is concrete, cracked and shiny with age, just like on the lower levels. The four windows at the front of the building and the four at the back are huge rectangles, set high in the walls, and covered by discolored crooked blinds that are older than I am. When I want to turn on the air conditioner, I have to drag a chair to the window and stand on it in order to reach the control. I only go to the trouble on hot summer nights.

I suppose if I'm going to continue to live here I really should fix the place up, but I don't have the kind of energy I once had. Besides, it's not like I'm ever going to invite guests up here.

I can't think about Pard's guns without also thinking about the cash he left behind. What I really need is a second safe, a secure storage provision here, in my private area, to hold guns and money.

And this realization reminds me how I've been feeling vulnerable lately. Too many people know I live in this big building by myself. The current security system only covers the shop floors. On this floor all I have to keep bad guys out are forty-year-old dead bolts on the interior and exterior doors. The exterior door opens to a landing and a rickety staircase that descends to an empty unlit alley. And the interior door to my apartment is located on the second floor, which means the stairwell is a dark gaping hole in the middle of my home. And this hole is empty and creepy at night, a source of nightmares.

A knock on the alley door makes me jump. The guns are arranged across my table like tokens in a morbid game.

'Just a minute,' I call. With no wasted movement, I transfer the guns to the broad bottom drawer of the dresser, nestling them atop my few pairs of jeans. Then I open the door.

< 30 >

It's Don's first wife, Nicole. There's not a person on the planet I'd rather not see more. And oh great, standing right behind her is Lizzie, Don's twelve-year-old daughter, who came out of the wreck with a broken wrist and a scratch on her neck from where the seat belt grabbed her, while my lovely twin babies – belted haphazardly because Don was careless and lazy and couldn't be bothered to do it properly – were flung and banged and broken.

'Nicole. What are you doing here?' I glance down at the back parking area to see a generic silver sedan parked crookedly across two slots. Texas plates, a rental.

Determined to prove that she's an artist, Nicole exudes a bohemian aura. With exaggerated gestures and wild brown hair, she wears colorful flowing skirts, embroidered tops, and crinkled scarves. She's added a delicate piercing at the crease of a nostril since the last time I saw her. The artsy mien is meant to distract from her uglier traits; she's promiscuous, manipulative, undependable, self-absorbed, and inconsiderate. On the other hand, she's easy enough to get along with. The trick is to smile and nod until she goes away. And she always goes away.

'Jessica, my darling, how are you?' A hugger, she steps close, wraps her arms around me, and squeezes for way too long. With my arms trapped at my sides and my lanky form bowed to fit her petite one, I endure.

When released, I open the door further and gesture them inside. Lizzie is pulling a medium-sized wheeled suitcase. Without a word, I take the suitcase from her and roll it back out to the landing before closing the door.

'How did you find me?' I ask.

'Where else would you have gone except home?'

She and Lizzie come to a halt in the middle of the floor. They look around.

< 31 >

'Not exactly a traditional abode,' Nicole says.

'Why are you here?' I ask again.

'I've been given an opportunity.'

'Good for you.' I don't want to hear how her life has taken a pleasant turn.

'I've been invited to study in Tuscany for two months.'

By study, I assume she's referring to her painting. I know nothing about art. She claims she has talent.

'How nice for you.'

'I need you to take Lizzie for the summer.' No one else in the world would have the audacity.

'We're not relatives, Nicole. I have no responsibility toward her whatsoever.' I'm uncomfortable having this conversation in front of Lizzie, who assesses me with her father's brown eyes, eyes wrenchingly similar to Cassie and Christy's.

When Don was alive Nicole dropped Lizzie off any time she pleased. She seldom gave notice and she never returned when she said she would. I can't count the number of weekend plans that had to be abandoned or the number of times one of us had to drive Lizzie clear across town to her school on weekday mornings because Nicole didn't show up as promised. It wasn't Lizzie's fault and I was careful never to let my resentment show. But that was before the accident and I don't think I have it in me to be kind when what I want to do is rant and screech. That's what happens when the person you're furious with is dead – there's no place to put your rage.

'You were a second mother to her.'

'Out of necessity.'

'How can you say that? She's part of your family. She and your daughters had the same father.'

The mention of my babies is a stab to my heart. No one

< 32 >

talks to me about my babies. No one. Especially the mother of the child who survived.

'She absolutely is not part of my family. I have no family.'

'It'll just be for a couple of months. Just for the summer.'

'I'm having enough trouble taking care of myself right now.' I won't tell this insensitive woman who's never known loss how difficult it is for me to get out of bed, to put one foot in front of the other, to pull air in and push it back out.

'Please.'

'No.' I walk to the door, open it, and wave them out.

Nicole's whole body signals her displeasure. She straightens her shoulders and draws an affronted breath; then she slumps in defeat and sighs; next she scuffs to the door like a thwarted teenager. Lizzie follows, head humbly bowed. When Nicole's beside me, she stops, turns tearful eyes toward me, and places her warm hand on my arm.

'You're one of my dearest friends,' she says. 'Please don't turn us away like this.'

'You two have a nice summer,' I tell her.

As soon as they're on the landing I close the door. I don't move until I hear the car pull away.

When I open the door, wanting to witness the disappearing brake lights of the rental car as it turns the corner, it's to find Lizzie sitting on the top step, suitcase next to her like it's her buddy. I'm not surprised.

< 33 >

Don's First Daughter

With Nicole's thick brown hair, full lips, perfectly tilted nose, and Don's heavily lashed deer eyes, Lizzie is a noticeably attractive child. Claiming one of the kitchen chairs, she drags it away from the table and sinks into it, fixing her eyes on the roses. Her hand finds its way to the table. She's clutching her cell phone so desperately that her knuckles are white.

My day was supposed to be about storing firearms. Now it's about taking care of a kid. I pull out the other chair and extract my phone from my pocket. Calling a furniture rental place, I order a twin-sized bed and a four-drawer chest to be delivered this afternoon between four and six.

'Did she leave you any money?' I ask.

Lizzie extracts an envelope from the outside pocket of her suitcase and places it on the table. Thinking it's probably a check to cover expenses, I open it to find a two-page document assigning me temporary guardianship of Elizabeth Marie Hockley. It's signed by Nicole and dated yesterday. There's a name I don't recognize scrawled across the witness line. The line for my signature is blank. Mainly it gives me the right to sign for medical treatment for Lizzie. There's also contact information – an address in Italy and a phone number. No money. I toss the papers on the table.

'In a little while we'll do some research into what activities

< 34 >

are going on here for kids your age during the summer.' My tight voice reveals my difficulty in controlling my anger. Nicole's fault, I remind myself, not Lizzie's.

Her phone gives a ding. She looks at the screen, begins texting madly.

While I'll admit our past relationship was colored by my disdain toward Nicole, I didn't dislike Lizzie – though at times I saw traces of the mother in the child. But because she was Don's child and not mine, when she was around I made it a rule that he was around, too. I wasn't going to entertain his kid while he played golf. And I haven't seen her in almost two years. I have no idea what she's into these days.

She finishes her text, places her phone on the table, then looks at her lap and sighs. My memories fuel mistrust. I once caught her going through my closet; and another time, after she'd been at the house, Christy's pink monkey was missing. I've been around the vendors too long; I'm becoming as suspicious as they are.

'Tennis? Swimming? Acting class?' I ask. 'There'll be loads of options. It'll be an opportunity to explore new interests. Caprock is proactive when it comes to keeping children busy during the summer.' Or at least it used to be when I was a kid. I realize that I sound frantic as I push these ideas at her, but the notion of her being constantly underfoot fills me with apprehension.

She looks up at me with tears in her lovely brown eyes, pain all over her face.

'What?' A few seconds ago she seemed resigned to being dumped by her mother. Now she's crying.

'I'm sorry.' Her whisper is a contrivance, forcing the listener to lean close and focus.

'It's not your fault.'

< 35 >

'Not about this.' She spreads her arms, indicating the current situation. 'About Daddy and Cassie and Christy. I never got a chance to tell you.'

I cringe at the names of my lost ones. She lost a father and two sisters. I lost a husband and two babies. I have no desire to bond with her over our pain. As the adult, am I supposed to console her? I simply don't have it in me.

'It should have been me,' she says woefully. 'I should have died, not them.'

'Wow. You're more like your mother than I realized.' My words and tone are mean and I really don't care. 'A man and two babies die and you're making it about you? Get over yourself.'

Her sorrowful expression morphs into a guarded one. Obviously she thought she was playing to a more gullible audience.

'I mean it, Lizzie. I will not tolerate manipulative bullshit, so put all your little tricks on hold while you're with me or I'll call whatever agency deals with abandoned children.' It's not an empty threat. If this doesn't work out, that's exactly what I'm going to do. 'Now, I've got errands to run and you're coming with me. Get up, let's go.'

Now that I've got a child in my zone, getting storage space for Pard's guns has advanced to the slot of top priority.

Grabbing her phone, she follows me down the interior stairs all the way to the first floor, where I unlock the front door. Her phone emits at least three text dings between the top and ground floors. It's an annoying sound. I'll have to find a way to pry that phone out of her pink little fingers.

Having let themselves in through the back, Emily and Thomas are the first ones here. We come across them as they toddle toward their booth, two slow-moving jowly elderlies who claim to sell books and magazines, but in

< 36 >

all honesty hardly ever sell anything. Like a small library, their area is given over to bookcases holding mostly old paperbacks that would be redeemed for a quarter at Half-Price Books, but are marked four and five dollars in Emily and Thomas's booth. Most of their area is taken over by dusty collections of out-of-date encyclopedias. Who would want an encyclopedia that's no longer true? They do have a few first editions that they keep locked in a glass-fronted cabinet – a complete set of Nancy Drew mysteries and a couple of Yerbys and Costains.

As old people often are, they're thrilled to see a young face.

'Who is this pretty thing?' Emily asks, honing in on Lizzie like she's found treasure.

'Hello there!' Thomas also gravitates toward the girl. 'Where did you spring from?'

Lizzie stands still, the way kids are trained to do when an unknown dog approaches.

'This is Lizzie,' I say. 'She'll be staying with me for a while.'

'Niece, cousin, daughter of a friend – who is she?' Emily wants to be the first to know. She reaches out a gnarled hand as if to stroke Lizzie's smooth cheek. Lizzie turns anxious eyes to me and I step between her and Emily.

'We've got errands to run,' I say. 'You two have a good day.'

I assume the best place to look for a weapons safe is a hunting store. Guns & Gear is just up the highway, and it turns out they have a generous selection. Presented with twelve options, I decide on a Steelwater with a twenty-two-gun capacity. The safe costs one thousand one hundred and seventy-five dollars, plus one-twenty for the high security lock and fifteen ninety-nine apiece for four racks – but hey,

< 37 >

the dehumidifier's free and if there's ever a fire, it's guaranteed to withstand for an hour. Since the guns and money were Pard's, I use his cash to pay for it. It'll be delivered this afternoon during the same time frame as the furniture.

At JC Penney we select bedding. I invite Lizzie to choose the color – she mutely points to blue, thank God; if she'd decided on pink I would have had to overrule. She's busy with her phone the whole time.

'Who're you texting?'

'Friends.'

When we return to the building I need to do some work in the office. I can't allow Lizzie to be alone upstairs until I've got the guns locked away, so I set her up with the old boxy computer on the desk while I work on the opposite side on the laptop.

'Look up Caprock summer programs,' I tell her.

Subdued and obedient, she slides into the chair and does as instructed, dividing her attention between the computer and her phone.

I immediately get caught up in business. There are seven inquiries from people interested in renting booths in my building – recent retirees, every one. I respond by inviting them to drop by, and I attach the standard guidelines for proceeding. One of the would-be vendors has a collection of over four hundred handmade dolls. I make a bet with myself that she prices them at over a hundred dollars apiece.

Then I, too, look up summer programs, just so I have an idea of the schedules and what the costs are going to be.

After an hour or so I realize that Lizzie hasn't shifted or even released a sigh since she sat down. The only communication between us since I snapped at her earlier was when she told me she was texting friends.

'Look,' I say, 'we're going to have to get along. This is

< 38 >

going to be a long and miserable summer if you're not going to talk to the person who's in charge of feeding you and taking you places.'

Her eyes meet mine as she takes up her phone and taps in a message, which makes me think whatever she's sending off is spiteful and about me. She returns her attention to the computer, but then she wiggles and opens her mouth like she has something to say, then she closes it again.

'What?' I ask.

'For someone in charge of feeding me, you're not doing a very good job.'

Good heavens. It's one-thirty. There was a time when I was fond of food, when I took pleasure in planning meals and grocery shopping. These days I find no pleasure in eating. With no refrigerator and no stove, how am I supposed to feed this kid?

'What do you usually eat for lunch?'

She shrugs, turns back to the screen, clicks the mouse.

'Have you found anything interesting?'

Another shrug. Her phone gives a ding.

I circle the desk and look over her shoulder.

She's got tabs on three places that offer riding lessons.

'Riding? As in riding a horse?'

'We're in Texas. It's what people here do.'

'I was thinking more along the lines of tennis or golf.'

She sighs.

'What?'

'You said I could explore new things and do what I'm interested in.' She collapses back in her chair, emitting a disgruntled snort as she crosses her arms over her chest. 'I should have known better. Nobody ever means what they say.'

Manipulation through guilt. And there's not a thing I can do about it because she's right. I did imply exactly that.

< 39 >

'Let's see what you've got.'

She calls up one of the places – Richardson Riding Academy, located thirty miles west of town.

Fifty bucks for an hour lesson, and that's if you have your own horse and board it with them. If you use one of their horses, it's sixty-five. The sessions are semi-private and, during the summer for a beginner, this particular school recommends three lessons a week. Plus the kids are expected to groom the horses, care for the tack, and muck out the stables.

Tennis lessons are also three weekly – at forty bucks a week. Swimming is even more reasonable – a month of daily morning classes for seventy-five dollars total. The library is offering creative writing classes for free. And the art department at the junior college is holding drawing classes – also at no charge.

'Riding lessons would cost a hundred and ninety-five dollars a week. Swimming lessons go every day and they cost less than twenty a week.'

Raised voices are coming from out in the building. I cock an ear, thinking there might be trouble – but no; it's just two of the vendors who don't hear well trying to communicate.

'I already know how to swim.'

'You can always learn to swim better. Also, it's healthy.'

'You're not going to let me do it.' She's a good pouter.

Tapping a quick multiplication into the calculator on my phone, the read-out gives me fifteen hundred and sixty. I show Lizzie the screen.

'That's how much eight weeks of riding lessons would cost,' I tell her. 'Do you have that kind of money? Because I sure don't.'

'You bought that stupid safe this morning.'

< 40 >

'So?'

'You had money to spend on that.'

I refuse to have this conversation. I guess someone laying out over thirteen hundred dollars in cash for a safe looked odd both to this kid and to the man behind the counter. I don't care.

'Come on,' I say. 'Let's go find you something to eat.'

On our way out of the building five old people stop us so they can meet Lizzie, call her darling and dear, and tell her how pretty she is.

< 41 >

The Principle

I have plenty of money. Lots, in fact. Don's life insurance, plus the sale of the house, left me well off. A fortune made from the death of my husband, my kids. It's still in our joint Dayton account. The thought of it makes me cringe.

While Don was alive he sent Nicole a sizeable monthly child-support check. But now that he's gone I imagine that's been reduced to a social security stipend. Nicole, art coming first, has always flitted from one part-time job to another. It strikes me that, financially, Nicole probably isn't doing well. If I were a better person this would stir my sympathy toward her daughter. It doesn't. There's a principle here. Lizzie isn't mine to support. And the tough reality is that she needs to learn to live the life she's been given.

I buy her a fast-food burger for lunch and then we go to the grocery store where I have her select a dozen cans of soup. In addition, I grab some wheat bread, peanut butter, and apples.

'Peanut butter and bread for breakfast, apples for snacks,' I tell her. 'The soup will be your lunch from now on.' When we get back home I show her where the can opener is, where the saucepan is, and how to use the hot plate. 'Wash your dishes and put them away when you're finished.'

'Where's the microwave?' she asks.

In response I spread my arms and look around. Is there

< 42 >

a microwave? Obviously not. All there is to my corner kitchen is a single counter with open shelves and a column of drawers, a sink, and the table.

'Could I get a job and earn the money for riding lessons?'

'Please, Lizzie, let it go. Getting you there and back would take up entire mornings. It's not going to happen.'

She looks like she's going to cry. How could she have become so attached to an idea that's only a couple of hours old? But her working isn't a bad idea. She could do chores for me. This is a vast building with public restrooms and lots of filthy corners. It would give her something to do.

When her phone gives another ding, drawing her attention, my control snaps.

'That phone has got to go.'

She clutches it to her breast like it's her baby. I close my eyes briefly, looking for empathy. She's away from home, away from her friends, dumped on her impatient step-mother. The phone is her connection to people who know and like her. The empathy doesn't come, but I do manage to find a ray of tolerance.

'Okay,' I tell her. 'Just – okay.'

When we return to my downstairs office there's a man waiting. Around fifty, with a shaved head, and glasses perched on his short plump nose, he introduces himself as Arthur Humboldt and holds out a business card. I accept it and give it a glance. He's an insurance adjustor from Las Vegas.

'Las Vegas?' I ask. 'What can I do for you?'

'I'm looking for this man.' He extracts a photo from an envelope and hands it to me. It's a picture of Raymond, Roxy's ex. The background is a restaurant. Raymond is wearing a bright floral shirt and smiling for the camera. He looks pleasant, not at all like the drunken grouch Roxy

< 43 >

made him out to be. 'His name's Raymond Verney. He's a friend of mine. His wife, Roxanne, works for you?'

'Ex-wife,' I tell him. 'Yes, I know Roxy Lynn. She doesn't work for me. She's one of the vendors. I'll take you to her.'

An insurance adjuster? What's this guy doing here? What's Roxy pulled me into?

Roxy's booth is on the exact opposite of the building, up near the front on the far wall. With Lizzie trailing, I lead Raymond's friend over several rows before taking a right turn. It's not long before he starts sneezing and sniffing. People with allergies suffer in here. Several of the vendors have carpets in their areas that have been down for as long as I can remember. And the carpets probably spent thirty years on previous floors before they were unrolled on to this one. The whole place smells of dusty mildew.

Roxy stands outside her counter chatting with Abe, who deals in rare coins. From what I've seen, Abe is more of a buyer than a seller. Permanently hunched, with only a couple of white hairs sprouting from the top of his head and liver spots all over his face, he must be ninety. And I bet he's made no will or statement of any kind declaring what he wants done with all his coins when he dies, which could happen any minute now.

Chest-high counters form one of the sides and the front barrier of Roxy's space. Sturdy partitions comprise the other side and the back. Mounted on these pseudo walls are trombones, saxophones, clarinets, snare drums; and between the instruments are musically themed decorations – notes and clef signs, sharps and flats made of cardboard. She used to change her decorations every couple of years, but these have been up for at least five and the once color-ful cut-outs are now so faded that their original color isn't discernible.

< 44 >

'Hey, Lizzie.' Inspired, I turn to her. 'You want to learn to play an instrument?'

She rolls her eyes.

I interrupt Roxy and Abe to introduce the visitor. Roxy's expression registers no surprise or alarm as she dryly acknowledges her relationship to Raymond.

'What do you want him for?' she asks. 'He owe you money?'

'No, no, nothing like that. We had a plan to meet up here in Caprock, that's all. He was supposed to call this morning, but he hasn't, and now I can't get hold of him.'

'I haven't seen him.'

'Will you let me know if you do?' He hands her one of his cards before pivoting toward the door. After taking a step, he turns back and tells me, 'You got a mold problem in here.'

His nose is red and his eyes are streaming.

'Yeah, I'll get right on that,' I say, a perfect combination of sarcasm and sincerity.

He sneezes as he walks away.

'What do you think that was about?' Roxy asks.

'It was about what he said it was about.'

'Think he suspects anything?'

She says this right in front of Lizzie and Abe. Eyes big with curiosity, Lizzie looks from me to Roxy and back to me again.

'Keep it to yourself, Roxy Lynn.' If I don't distract her, she's likely to blurt it all out. People her age no longer see value in discretion. So I ask, 'How old's your carpet? I'm thinking about instigating a new policy that if a carpet's over ten years old, it needs to be cleaned or removed.'

This gets the desired reaction. Both Roxy and Abe start blustering and bristling and accusing me of overstepping.

< 45 >

As Lizzie and I walk away the two of them are conspiring about getting up a petition to nullify any carpet guidelines I might have the audacity to try to enforce.

When we get back to the office there's a tiny gray woman waiting just outside the door. She steps forward, hand outstretched.

'Are you Jessica?' she asks as we shake hands. 'I'm Audrey Persons. A friend of Genevieve's.'

Genevieve operates a clothes concession on the second floor. She's got a collection of hats from the forties that are in exceptional condition. She's asking two hundred apiece for them, though, so it's unlikely they'll ever sell.

'Yes, I'm Jessica. How can I help?'

'Genevieve mentioned you recently had a booth come available?'

'Sure.' There's always a booth available. It's not like somebody has to die to make room. 'Come on in the office and I'll lay out the rules and responsibilities.'

We move into the office. I pull the standard rental form from the file drawer in my desk and hand it across to her, indicating that she should take the seat on the opposite side of the desk.

'You can go out on the floor and have a walk around,' I tell Lizzie, who's hanging by the door. She makes no move, so I say, 'Or you can stay here.'

But there's no chair for her. She continues to stand and I know this hovering of hers, the way she's always there, is going to make me insane. And then her phone gives a text ding, and I know that's going to make me insane, too.

The woman clears her throat and I turn my attention to her.

'What merchandise will you be selling?' I ask. We've already got several dealers in jewelry, furniture, and household items.

< 46 >

'Urns.'

This I haven't heard before.

'Urns? For ashes?'

'Oh yes. When someone dies their loved one keeps their ashes in an urn. And the remains are cherished for a while, kept on the mantle or on the table beside the bed.' She's got a whole story going on in her head. 'But time moves forward and the guardian of the urn dies and what do you think happens then?'

Baffled, I shake my head.

'I buy them. They can be recycled, you know. And there are urns for pets, too.'

'How much does one of your urns go for?'

'Starting at a hundred.'

'Alrighty then.' Used urns. At least she won't be taking business away from any of the other vendors. I push my chair from the desk and stand. 'Let's go take a look at the available space.'

We walk from the office and Lizzie follows.

'You're such a beautiful girl,' my new tenant tells Lizzie, who preens and smiles modestly, easily slipping into the role she'll be playing all summer.

< 47 >

Midnight Conversation

New urns online are priced between a hundred and a hundred-fifty. And the new vendor intends to start pricing her used ones at a hundred.

It's not my business what these people charge for their stuff as long as they pay their rent.

For dinner I feed Lizzie what I feed myself – salad from the grocery store salad bar and scrambled eggs. She seems okay with it and later falls asleep in front of the television. I nudge her awake and wave her toward her bed, which I placed in the corner as far from my sleeping area as possible. Privacy through distance.

Sylvia (decorative furniture, first floor) has a couple of oriental screens – reproductions, not authentic. I wonder how much she wants for them.

I've been waiting for Lizzie to go to sleep so I can transfer the guns to the safe, which I had the delivery guys center along the front wall. A large and jarring addition to my environs, it's been drawing my eye all evening. As soon as Lizzie's been motionless for fifteen minutes, I carefully retrieve the firearms from the drawer where I tucked them this morning. I place them in the safe, set up the combination, close the heavy door, then go to bed. But I can't sleep. I'm fixated on Pard's money in the safe downstairs. It's perfectly secure there, but Pard's money should be with

< 48 >

Pard's guns. And I want them both to be with me, up here in my new safe.

I'm not going to be able to relax until I fetch the cash. I kick back the sheets, slip on my flip-flops, and drag my gray sweater over the sleeves of my pajamas. Because I don't want to announce to the world that I'm walking around the empty building by myself at midnight, I don't turn on the overhead lights. I grab a flashlight, but I don't turn it on either.

I trudge all the way down the two flights of stairs and back to the office, making the whole journey in the ambient light that slants in through the front window. And then, as though this small amount of activity has exhausted me, I drop into my chair and simply sit there.

Sometimes I tell myself I'm doing something for one reason, but it turns out I'm doing it for another. Right now, for instance. This hike downstairs isn't about fetching money. It's about urns.

I unlock the safe and, bending and reaching to the bottom back corner, take out one of the urns – my mother's. The other two that I also keep in there – Don's and the girls' (together in death as they were at birth) – well, I'm just not ready. Mom's is the only one I can bear to look at. Cold in my hands, it's an elegant amphora of pale blue porcelain. I place it in the center of the desk and once again sink into the chair.

'That stupid Nicole showed up today,' I say to my mother's urn. 'She dumped Lizzie on my doorstep. You remember Lizzie, Don's daughter from his first marriage. Who does something like that?'

Before the memorial service in Dayton, when she stood by my side as I sobbed over the loss of my loved ones, I hadn't seen Mom for a year. She and Don didn't get along.

< 49 >

'He's stuffy and exacting,' she said during her first visit to us in our new home. 'He follows you around redoing everything you do, as though you can't fold a dishtowel properly or center a picture frame.'

Likewise, he had nothing good to say about her.

'She's flighty and her priorities make no sense,' he said later that same evening. 'Why is she so dedicated to those people in her building who aren't her responsibility? What could possibly be in it for her?'

Now I know. The money they left behind.

She was right about him. Don liked every item to be in its place, and he expected the people around him to behave appropriately and predictably.

But he was wrong about her. There was nothing flighty about Mom. She was cautious and shrewd, and she picked her battles carefully. She would never have been dragged into this mess of Roxy's.

She visited again when the twins were born, staying for a week that was made tense by the fact that Don was obviously avoiding her. He left early for work and stayed late. And when he was around he made no effort to be friendly, but went directly to his office and stayed there.

'He makes me feel like an interloper,' she said.

I couldn't dispute it because it was true.

'The two of you got off on the wrong foot, that's all,' I told her.

It was a time of unhappy enlightenment. The two people closest to me, both of whom I loved, had nothing but contempt for one another.

'If your girls want to get to know their granny, you're going to have to bring them to Caprock,' she said as I took her to the airport. 'I won't be coming here again.'

I understood and agreed. Who needed the tension?

< 50 >

Promising to make a yearly trip, I gave her a quick good-bye hug, and she disappeared inside the terminal. The next time I saw her, the girls and Don were gone. When I got word that she'd died of an aneurism, I was still too numb from the first loss to pay much attention to the second. And now her charred remains are stored in this container, her death hardly marked by her only child. She would've been the best grandmother.

'Have you run across Roxy Lynn's ex-husband up there? No, of course not. From what she says of him, he went the other direction.'

Why do I assume my mother is in heaven? Isn't heaven only for religious people? She was definitely not that. I believe my babies are in heaven. Don, I have my doubts about. No, that's not fair. Like Mom, Don wasn't a church-goer, but he was a good man, bighearted when it came to his employees at the bank, patient with the twins, support-ive toward me. He could be picky about trivial matters, and he was egocentric, but who doesn't think of themselves first? On the other hand, I suspect his selfishness was the reason he didn't buckle the twins in properly. He was in a hurry because he was late for his scheduled tee time, and he resented having to taxi Lizzie around. Maybe someday I'll forgive him enough to wish him well in the afterlife.

'The new woman who's going to rent the front corner of the basement plans to sell used urns. We had better loca-tions, but it's the one she wanted. And the urns – she's got to empty them before she can sell them, right? So I'm wondering what she does with the ashes.'

Mom purchased this building thirty-two years ago, so it was part of my childhood. I don't know her motives in becoming the proprietor of an antique mall, though I guess it gave her autonomy. A bit of a rebel, she wasn't one to

< 51 >

take orders. I thought there'd be time to have this conversation, that someday we'd put our feet up and sip wine as she explained to me what was going through her head when she bought this building that housed the stuff of these obsessive elderly nut-jobs.

I'm distracted by a noise coming from out on the floor. I assume it's Lizzie, come looking for me. I rise from the desk and cross to the door.

'Lizzie?' I call her name softly, unwilling to disturb the night.

There's no answer.

From the doorway the sound is a bit louder, clearer. And there's a rhythm to it. *Shhhh-haa, Shhhh-haa.*

I follow the noise, turning right from the office, then left at the aisle.

Three booths up, Laurence Penn is lying on his back on a rollaway bed. I shine the flashlight at him, illuminating his profile. His big nose and sharp chin poke upward, giving him the exaggerated features of a troll. This proximate, the snoring is ungodly. What's he doing here? Nestled into the juncture of his arm is a framed photograph of his wife, Lydia, who died six months ago.

Lydia and Laurence worked this booth together for twenty-three years. They opened it right after they retired from their jobs as teachers. Christmas decorations. This is one of the most profitable enterprises in the building. Everybody loves Christmas. And everybody loves Laurence, who knows every verse to every Christmas carol, even the most obscure ones.

Just beyond his snoring form is an eight-foot-high bookcase with ten shelves; and each shelf is packed with Santas of every race and from every era. More shelved cabinets mark the perimeter of his area. On display are snow globes,

< 52 >

miniature decorated villages, sleighs, tiny carolers, crosses, stars, mangers, wise men, tree ornaments, and wreaths. As always, when I'm in this booth, I experience a yearning for some fulfillment, some sort of awareness or knowledge that's so vague, so ephemeral, that I can't even put a name to it.

Because women tend to live longer, there are twice as many women in our community as there are men. Ordinarily when a man loses his wife the women swoop in. Casseroles are offered several times a week, laundry is whisked away and returned fresh and ironed, groceries are supplied, advice is given. But that hasn't happened with Laurence and I'm not sure why. I go back to the office, write 'L – See me. Jess' on a sticky note and, returning to the booth, place the note across the picture of Lydia's round face.

Back in the office I return Mom's urn to the safe. Then I transfer Pard's cash from the box with his name on it to a box with no name. I return his empty box to the safe and, holding the unlabeled one in front of my chest like a shield, take it with me. Laurence's snore stays in my ears all the way to the second floor. It doesn't fade until I close the door at the bottom of my stairs.

< 53 >

Joe Stops By

In the morning Lizzie has her peanut butter on bread, brushes her teeth, and gets dressed. Then she sits at the table and silently watches. She watches as I make a cup of tea, as I straighten my bed, as I gather my clothes and take them into the bathroom. When I emerge, she's still there, big eyes following. Even without the resentment that's an inherent factor of our relationship, I'd still find her the most annoying being alive.

Also, she's fastened her hair back with a regular rubber band, which'll cause hair breakage, which means I'll have to buy her some insulated hair ties. This need for an insignificant hair accessory reminds me how much kids cost, how much upkeep they require. And this makes me furious at Nicole all over again. Really – how could she have done this?

Downstairs, on the way to unlock the front door, I lead Lizzie on a detour past Laurence's area. Laurence is gone and there's no sign of the rollaway. Lizzie's fascinated with the contents of the booth. She steps to the center and turns a complete circle, arms open as though she wants to gather it all in for a big hug.

'Look at all this Christmas stuff,' she says. She's a pretty girl and her delighted grin would melt most hearts. But not mine.

< 54 >

'Time to open up,' I tell her, moving away.

I unlock the front door to find Joe waiting on the sidewalk. The navy suit is unattractive and ill fitting. Off the rack at Walmart would be my guess. My mind flashes to the beautiful suits that lined Don's closet. I rein in my thoughts.

'Man clothes can be so lacking in style,' I say, by way of a greeting.

'As always, your opinion warms my heart.'

'I assume that's required work-wear?'

'Yup. I'm here to inspect Pard's booth.' When Lizzie comes up beside me, he asks, 'Who's this?'

'Lizzie, say hi to Joe, a police detective who suspects one of our recently departed of nefarious activity – which absolutely isn't the case.'

I push the door open further, waving Joe inside. Sniffing and peering suspiciously into the front booths, he immediately releases two sneezes.

'You got some kind of airborne allergen in here,' he says.

'So I've been told. Come on up.'

The three of us troop up the stairs to Pard's booth. None of the vendors have shown up yet, so the building is empty and our footsteps hit hard on the stairs, reverberating to the farthest corners.

'A lot of his items have already been claimed,' I tell him. 'But hey, you can ask anyone and they'll tell you who got what, because believe me, they pay attention.'

Pard's booth has a picked-over look. The best of the smaller items have gone away, leaving only dented pots, hard-used tools, and small pieces of splintery furniture. Across the aisle, Carly has claimed two chamber pots, which she's filled with tenth-generation silk flowers and set on opposite ends of her counter. A couple of washboards lean against the back wall of Barry's booth. He specializes

< 55 >

in turntables and jukeboxes. I can't imagine why he'd want washboards.

'Go ahead,' I tell Joe. 'Poke around.'

As he strolls into the depths of Pard's area, I catch sight of movement in the rear shadows of Barry's booth. Barry pokes his head out from behind the barrier that separates the front section from the back. It's unusual for him to be here so early. Most days he's not here until eleven. His hair's poking up and his chin is rough with yesterday's whiskers.

Did he spend the night here, too? Am I inadvertently running a dormitory for old men?

Joe looks behind shelves and under tables. He shifts the larger items and opens the door of an old icebox. He approaches the back cabinet and pulls the knobs of the drawer where Pard stored the handguns. He sniffs. The next inhalation is a good long nose-search. I should have done something about the machine odor of that drawer. He closes the drawer and straightens.

'This is it? This is all he left behind?'

'Yep.'

'Okay, then. If you hear anything, let me know.' He steps from Pard's area and turns toward the stairs.

'Hey,' I rush after him, 'I want to ask a favor. A man from Las Vegas showed up here looking for the ex-husband of one of my vendors.'

'And you're telling me this, why?'

'I wonder if you'd mind checking him out. Roxy's old and fragile and his questions really upset her.'

'What is it you're asking, exactly?'

'I'm asking you, as a favor, to see if there are any warrants out for him or if he's a convicted felon. The people in this building are old and easily frightened and it doesn't take much to get them worked up.'

< 56 >

'Did he give you a contact number?'

'I've got it in the office.'

'And what's the name of the fellow he was looking for?'

'Raymond Verney.' Why did I tell him? I didn't think, that's why. Now he's got a connection between the two men in his head.

We troop down to the office. I give him Humboldt's card and see him to the door, with Lizzie trailing.

'What was he looking for?' Lizzie asks as we watch him get in his car.

Her query penetrates to an area of my psyche that's been dormant for quite a while – my conscience. At one point in my life morality was a constant, not a principle to be discarded or ignored. But these days I find right and wrong to be subjective. And if a twelve-year-old girl stands at my side, watching everything I do and everything the people around me do – well, I simply don't give a damn.

Out in the parking lot, Marlina pulls up, gets out of her car, and gives a wave, signaling for us to wait. I open the door for her.

'Hey,' she says. 'Genevieve said we got some woman opening a recycled urn booth.'

'Her name's Audrey Persons,' I say. 'You'll like her.'

'What do you think she does with the ashes?'

'Do we really want to know?'

'And you, little girl, what are you doing with your summer?' Marlina beams, thrilled to see a face with no wrinkles, a form that's straight, and eyes that are bright with energy instead of dulled by arthritic pain.

Lizzie shrugs and looks charmingly shy. She's going to be a big hit with these susceptible seniors.

'Because if you'd like to earn some money, I've got a few things need doing in my booth.'

< 57 >

And as easy as that, I'm rid of my irksome shadow. Lizzy follows Marlina up the stairs and I don't see her for two hours. I spend the time toying with temptation. The keys to the boxes are in the right middle drawer. I contemplate the vendors that correspond with each box, speculating about the amounts stored eight feet from where I sit.

Carly pops her head in the door.

'Marlina's got that girl of yours removing every plate and pitcher and dusting the shelves.'

I recoil when she refers to Lizzie as my girl.

'How much is she paying her?'

'Two dollars an hour.' Figures. Stuck in the last century, stingy Marlina probably thinks that's a fair wage.

Having tattled, Carly disappears.

Marlina is the most tight-fisted of all the vendors. She also has a locked box in the safe. Mom may have promised never to snoop, but I made no such promise. Closing the office door, I cross to the safe, extract Marlina's box, and return to the desk. Marlina's key is easy enough to dig out. I insert it, give a twist, remove the lock, and lift the lid.

Good Lord.

I flick through the piles of bills – mostly hundreds and fifties. A rough count tells me there's at least fifty thousand dollars in here. I rifle to the bottom of the box, looking for a will or some sort of statement about what Marlina wants done with all this money. Some of these people don't have family – but most have relatives somewhere. Children, children of children, children's children's children. If not direct descendants, what about siblings, nieces, nephews? I've heard Marlina mention grandkids in Kentucky. And here this money sits, with no instruction pertaining to its allocation when she dies.

< 58 >

There's a knock on the door.

'Just a minute.' I snap the lid closed, click the lock in place, and rush around to cram the box in the safe. I turn toward the door. 'Come on in.'

'You left a note for me to come see you.' Saggy and gray, Laurence shuffles in like a kid in trouble with the teacher.

Circling to my side of the desk, I sit and motion him to come in and take the opposite chair.

'Why were you sleeping in your booth last night?'

He looks down, works his dry lips in and out. He's a gangly man and he'd looked so uncomfortable on that cot.

'Laurence. This is a place of business, not a domicile.'

'Lydia loved her Christmas things,' he says.

'Yes, she did. I guess you miss her.'

He nods, keeping his face turned toward his lap; and I know it's because he doesn't want me to see the tears in his eyes.

'You can't sleep here.'

He rises and scuffs out. Poor old guy.

I write this memo:

Concessionaires –

As of today any rugs that are over twenty years old must be cleaned or removed. You have a week to comply or I will see to their removal myself.

Anyone employing my young guest, Lizzie, will pay her, at the minimum, four dollars an hour.

Spending the night on the premises is not allowed.

Also, I'm advising that, should any of you be so inclined, I will happily keep documents such as wills or any other important paperwork on file in my office.

< 59 >

I read it through. I have mixed feelings about the last point. I might have smudged the line between right and wrong, but I have yet to disregard the line between idiocy and logic. The idea of these ancients not preparing for their own deaths rankles. On the other hand, it's not my business and I could get rich doing nothing but waiting for them to die.

I delete the last sentence before posting the notice on the bulletin board by the front door.

< 60 >

Return of Humboldt

All morning people poke their heads in to complain about me making up rules that have never been needed before. The person I don't hear from is Lizzie. When I wander the floors looking for her, I'm told that one of the vendors – Estelle, basement, toys – has taken her out to lunch. Good for Lizzie.

I trudge up the stairs to Barry's booth. He's perched on a stool behind his counter, glasses balanced on the end of his nose as he reads an electronics magazine.

'Did you sleep here last night?' I ask.

'I had a late delivery, so yeah, I bedded down in back.' He doesn't say what was being delivered, and I don't want to know.

'How late?'

'Two.'

'So you slept until two, then you let strangers in and out of the building, then you came back here and slept the rest of the night? Does this happen often?' By strangers I mean street thugs. I've been selectively naïve. I know what Barry does and who he deals with. Yet I haven't allowed myself to think about the timing of his illicit activities.

'Every once in a while.' Seeing that I'm disturbed, he says, 'Sometimes it's necessary. But don't worry – they're in and out and I lock the place up tight and reset the alarm.'

< 61 >

'I don't like it.'

The current alarm system is antiquated, and there's a lot of money in the safe. It's time for a security update. I've got to quit putting it off. Also, I need to start paying more attention to who's coming and going in the building.

'It's the way I've always done it.' Of course it is. 'Did you know there's a guy from Las Vegas going around the building asking questions about Raymond?'

Strange how a few days ago we would have referred to him as Roxy's ex, but now that we've had the intimate experience of placing his dead body in a country grave, we're on first-name terms.

'He was by yesterday. He's here now?' This is unsettling. 'I'll look into it. Tell me something – what possible use do you have for those washboards?'

'Just something to remember Pard by. He and I worked right next to each other for a lot of years.'

Humboldt has left a trail of disgruntled old folks in his wake. It doesn't take me long to track him down. He's with Sylvia, rear quarter, first floor.

A sweet-faced great-grandmother with an acquisitive soul, Sylvia runs estate sales. In addition to the fee she charges the deceased's family, she cherry-picks the higher-end items for her booth, never paying nearly what they're worth, and most times not paying anything at all. Dead people's treasures. It's a racket. She operates the largest concession on the premises. Every inch of her space holds high-quality furniture, and every surface is stacked with crystal, lamps, china, vases. Every drawer holds sets of silver and fine handmade linens. She's got more stuff than anybody.

Sylvia always reigns from behind the captain's desk at the rear center of her booth. That's where she is today.

< 62 >

Humboldt stands in front of her, rocking from one foot to the other, as she holds the picture of Raymond in her palm and studies it with a perplexed crease marring her brow. As I approach I pass by one of her decorative screens. Recalling the need for privacy in my living area, I glance at the price tag. Eight hundred ninety-five dollars. Twice the price of a new one online.

'This man's asking about Roxy Lynn's ex-husband,' she says, relieved by my arrival.

'Roxy told you yesterday he hasn't been around,' I tell him. 'Why are you back asking the same thing? And why are you asking people who don't even know him?'

'I'm worried about him, ma'am. He doesn't answer his phone. I've been asking people he used to know if they've seen him, but they can't tell me anything. His ex-wife is the only lead I have.' Same as yesterday, he's sniffing and coughing. He rubs his red eyes with a tissue.

'No, sir. This woman right here is not a lead. She and Roxy barely know each other.' Sylvia opens her mouth to protest, but I override her. 'And she knows nothing about Roxy's ex-husband.' I turn toward the front of the building, willing him to walk along with me. He complies, releasing several sneezes as I escort him to the door.

'You got a real dust and mold problem in here,' he says.

'I'm working on it. The place is full of filthy old rugs.' I open the door and motion him out. 'Mr. Humboldt, if questioning an elderly woman who doesn't even know the guy is your only path to follow, then you're good and lost.'

I watch as he crosses the parking lot. He makes some sort of gagging sound that's so loud I can hear it from inside. Then his shoulders heave as he aims and releases a glob of phlegm. I honestly have no feeling stronger than mild disdain toward him until that second. But the thought

< 63 >

of that splodge of slime out there on my property carries weight, and within me an intense dislike is born. He opens the driver's door of a silver Taurus with Nevada plates. I watch for a few minutes, but he doesn't drive away. The wind seems to have picked up.

Across the street a chubby dark man tiptoes through the lower level of the rubble mountain, picking up small items and dropping them into a large garbage bag. I've recognized some of the people scavenging over there, but this one doesn't look familiar. When is the city going to get that mess cleared? I guess there are crags of destruction all over town. They'll get to it when they get to it.

When I return to the office it's to find Lizzie sprawled in the visitor's chair, one knee cocked over the armrest, reading a paperback. Oh, that's good. I didn't know she was a reader. It'll help her pass the time until her mother comes back.

'What're you reading?'

She shows me the cover of the book. I recognize it from Emily and Thomas's booth. *Sweet Savage Love* by Rosemary Rogers, a bodice-ripper from the seventies. The picture on the front shows a woman with cascading golden curls; her large breasts spill over a partially laced corset, and she's being manhandled by a muscular pirate. Erotica before it was called erotica. Definitely not appropriate for a girl of twelve.

'They didn't charge you for that, did they?'

'Loaned it.' She returns her nose to the book.

I google security companies, pick one at random, and arrange for them to come in first thing tomorrow morning to install a new system.

A few minutes later Sylvia limps into the office, leaning heavily on her cane. In addition to having bad knees and

< 64 >

hips, her upper back is so humped that it rises above the back of her head. It's a wonder she can get around at all.

'Want to take me to Pard's house?' she asks. 'I want to take inventory of what he left behind.' She hasn't driven in years. One of her kids or grandkids drops her off every morning and picks her up in the late afternoon.

'Sure.' I, too, am curious about what's in Pard's house. 'You have a key?'

'No.'

'Then how are we going to get in?'

'We'll figure something out.' She eyes me like she thinks I'm an idiot, which I guess I am.

I get up from my chair. Grabbing her phone from the desk, Lizzie gets up like she's coming, too. My first thought is that she shouldn't come. But then I decide I don't care one way or the other. I'm not going to spend the summer sneaking around and hiding everything I do. The three of us go out to my car.

When I circle the block, driving past the front of the building, Humboldt's Ford's still parked out there, but he's not in it. Has he gone back inside to ask more questions?

I've never been to Pard's house before. I'd estimate it was built in the fifties. Austere and lacking any sign of comfort or welcome, it's a small wood-frame with peeling paint. I park out by the curb. The grass is brown and the elm is dry. Three steps lead to a covered porch that isn't even big enough for the three of us to stand on. Lizzie and Sylvia wait as I climb the steps, press the button, and hear the chime inside. As expected, no answer. Cupping my hands around my eyes, I peer through two layers of dirty glass – the storm door and the diamond-shaped window of the wooden front door. The outer door opens but the inner door is locked.

< 65 >

I hop off the porch. We crunch across the grass to the side of the house and head toward the back. The detached garage that marks the end of the driveway is tiny with an old-fashioned pull-up door. Curious, I grab the handle and lift. Not surprisingly, the garage is an extension of his booth. Anvils, milking stools, iceboxes, blacksmith tongs. There are a couple of mangles that look like they're in pretty good shape, and three horse plows.

'I'm going to need a bigger booth.' Sylvia's claiming it all for herself. She's going to start a war.

The back door is also locked.

'You can get in through here.' Indicating the adjacent window, Sylvia's so impaired by the curvature of her spine that she's unable to do more than peep over the sill.

She steps aside so I can remove the screen and prop it against the wall. Sliding the glass upward on its rough rails, I swing my leg over and duck inside. I'm in the kitchen. Sticking close, Lizzie enters the same way. I open the back door so Sylvia can hobble in. The house smells like Pard – greasy and rancid.

'Whose house is this?' Lizzie asks with a critical sniff.

'Pard's. He's the guy that died.'

'I guess that happens a lot with those people.'

'You'd think so. But so far, since I got here, it's just been Laurence's wife, Lydia, and Pard.'

'Laurence's wife died?'

'About six months ago.'

'I like Laurence. He loves Christmas. Why are we here?'

'Just poking around.'

The lower cabinets of the kitchen hold rows of wide shallow drawers. Sylvia begins opening the upper doors. Hands reaching high, it's a struggle for her to extract a single glass from the overhead cabinet. Instructing Lizzie

< 66 >

to stay and help Sylvia, I move into the living room. Faded curtains hang limply at the windows. The frame of the couch lists to one side, and there's a dent in the end cushion that's in the shape of Pard's skinny butt. An entire wall is done up in dull paneling, and the television is a huge box. I bet it's been twenty years since he invested in any sort of renovation or bought something new for his home.

Beyond the living room is a hallway with two bedrooms and a bathroom. One of the rooms is obviously Pard's, with a queen-sized bed, a dresser, and clothes that I recognize in the closet. The other is full of – of all things – typewriters through the ages. There are too many to count, representing every era; there are at least three Remington Portables. Coronas, Fords, Royals – all elegant, more beautiful and mysterious than I'd expect office machinery to be. Sylvia shuffles up behind me.

'Would you look at this?' Her tone is worshipful, like she's seen God.

'He could've sold these in his booth.'

'Different era, different stock. He would've had to change his theme completely.'

'But still.'

Ancient eyes sparkling with avarice, she shuffles further into the room and starts to inspect the typewriters. In the corner is a gray shoulder-high file cabinet. Nosey, I approach it and open the top drawer.

Receipts, instruction manuals, insurance papers, owner's manuals, medical records.

Next drawer, more of the same.

There are four drawers stuffed with out-of-date paperwork. There are no dividers, no labels or folders. I reach into the middle of a middle drawer and pull out a warranty for a refrigerator purchased in 1962. I toss it back in and

< 67 >

pull out a folded sheet – a claim slip for watch repair dated October 10, 1981.

'Sylvia, you wouldn't believe all this.'

'Hmm.' She can't be bothered to look away from the cherished booty. She's making plans for those typewriters.

'He's got an auto repair bill for a Studebaker in 1968. Why would he keep this?'

'Pard saved everything.' She says it critically, like she doesn't do the same thing.

This useless paperwork might come in handy. I grab a handful of the receipts and warranties and slip them into the side pocket of my purse.

Leaving Sylvia to ponder and scheme, I return to the kitchen. Lizzie, hearing my approach, slams the drawer she's rifling through and turns toward me. I was a school-teacher. I recognize sneaky guilt.

'What did you find?' I ask, on alert.

'Nothing.'

I shoot her my skeptical look, but stop there. She's not my kid and she's not my student. If she's got a secret, so what?

Sylvia shambles in. Her frail arms strain to support an Underwood typewriter, an elegant machine, black keys trimmed in gold. Her cane dangles uselessly from a finger. She's misshapen and poorly balanced; it's only a matter of time before the weight of the typewriter causes her to topple.

'I have to take something out of here with me,' she says, helpless in the throes of her grasping nature.

'You have no right to Pard's stuff, you know.' I move forward and hold out my arms, inviting her to unload her burden.

'First come, first served.'

< 68 >

'The others'll never put up with it.'

'What they don't know won't hurt them.'

'What happened to all of you splitting everything?'

'They snooze, they lose.'

'I never realized how heavily you rely on clichés.'

It'll be interesting to see how this progresses.

As soon as I'm back at the office, I slip the paperwork I took from Pard's into the empty box in the safe that has his name on it.

< 69 >

To Flourish Wrongly

It takes three hours for the security people to install the system. When the men leave, and the new locks and alarms are installed on the bottom floors and my upstairs living area, I feel much better.

Sherman appears in my office doorway.

'Why'd you change the alarm system?' Defensive and belligerent. 'You can't deny us access.'

'I'm not going to. I'll give the new code to anyone who asks. But you have to sign out a key card when you're coming in during off-hours.'

'We've always been free to come and go as we please.'

'And you still are. It's just that now you have to think ahead.'

'You don't see the contradiction in that?' He heads off to spread the word. I'm going to be listening to complaints about this all day.

Ken arrives. 'Sylvia's got a whole new inventory,' he says. 'Old typewriters. Know anything about that?'

'Not my business.'

What did she do, get her kids to burgle Pard's for her during the night?

'And another thing – Pard kept a box in your mom's safe. Whatever's in there should be evenly divided, just like the contents of his booth.'

< 70 >

I disagree. That safe is mine, and when someone dies without leaving further instructions, whatever's in there belongs to me and me alone. But still, disclosure seems called for, even if it's bogus. I'm pleased that I anticipated this; the timing couldn't have been better. On the other hand, it's not all that hard to stay a step ahead of people who can't walk without canes.

'I forgot all about it.' Up until my life fell apart I never lied. These days lies come easily. 'Let's see what's in there.'

I cross to the safe, remove Pard's box, and return to the desk. Placing it in the center, I make a show of searching for the key, finding it, inserting it. I lift the lid carefully, like I'm concerned the contents might jump out at me.

'It's just a bunch of his worthless old paperwork,' Ken says, emitting a derisive snort.

I lift out the top sheet. It's a receipt for a Westinghouse oven's heating element from 1972. I offer it for his inspection.

'Why would he keep all this?' I ask.

'He kept everything.' His judgmental tone exactly matches Sylvia's. Do these people not see themselves?

Ken goes away.

I make my way to Sylvia's booth. Sure enough, the typewriters that were in Pard's spare bedroom are now placed throughout her area. Surfaces that were already cluttered with vases, lamps, and pitcher-and-bowl sets are now even more tightly packed in order to make room for the typewriters.

Sylvia is, as usual, behind her desk. She gives me a smug smile. I shake my head, shrug, and return to the office.

Ten minutes later Barry drops by to comment.

'Did Sylvia tell you where she got her new stock? Because I remember Pard mentioning that he had an antique typewriter collection.'

< 71 >

'Not my business,' I say again.

They've definitely got it figured out. I wonder if Sylvia's prepared.

When Estelle's head appears in the doorway, I dread hearing more of the same. But she offers a change of subject.

'You don't think it's in poor taste to have accouterments of death so close to my toy booth?'

Our dealer in used urns is in the process of moving in. She and her two grandsons have been making trips in and out and up and down all morning.

'Oh, it's categorically in poor taste.'

'So, what are you going to do about it?'

'Nothing.'

'What I want to know is – what does she do with the ashes that are already in those things?'

'Let me know when you find out.'

'Where's your little friend? I told her I'd take her to lunch and then I got some chores for her.'

'She's working in Laurence's booth.' Estelle goes off to find Lizzie.

Lizzie's been dusting Santas all morning. That's twelve more dollars for her stash. Last night it took ages for her to turn out her light. She was reading. The potboiler is substantial, I'd estimate seven hundred pages, and she's already a third of the way through it. I guess she's learning everything there is to know about lust and passion on the high seas.

After she went to sleep I went through her things. I was curious about that guilty drawer-slam at Pard's. She hasn't had time to really settle in so her hiding place was uninspired – the back corner of the bottom drawer of the dresser. The extreme reaction was about money. Folded in with the six bucks she got from Marlina is a fifty-dollar bill. So. She took fifty dollars from Pard's kitchen drawer.

< 72 >

Roxy shows up at the door. The beads around her neck and the studs in her ears perfectly match the green of her belt and shoes. At her age, where does she get the energy to care about color-coordinated accessorizing?

'That friend of Raymond's came back and asked me more of the same yesterday afternoon. And then he followed me home last night,' she says.

'That's not good.'

'I didn't notice him until I turned in at the house. He slowed down, then drove on past.'

'How could you not see him following you?' The last mile to her place is an untraveled two-lane road through flat land. Visibility goes forever in all directions.

'I would've if I'd been paying attention.'

She's too stooped and small to do much more than peek over the steering wheel, so I imagine her not noticing him was due more to her not being able to see the rearview mirror than it was to her not paying attention. Also, she's too old to live so far out of town by herself. Not my business. What is my business is that her mean squint when she talks about Humboldt is the same mean squint she had when she spoke of Raymond before she shot him.

'I know I said you could keep the Beretta for the week, but now I'm thinking you should return it sooner rather than later.'

She presses her lips together and does an about-face.

'I mean it, Roxy,' I call after her, 'I want it back first thing tomorrow.'

As soon as she's out of sight, I call Joe. He's not in so I leave a message: 'Did you find out anything about that guy I asked you about? Give me a call.'

Barry returns. 'I need the new alarm code and one of those key cards. I got business to tend to tonight.'

< 73 >

I give him what he needs and make a note that he's checked out a key.

Fifteen minutes later Joe shows up at my office. If that's not the same poorly fitting suit he was wearing yesterday, it's one just like it. Child-support payments, mortgage payments on the house he still owns with his ex-wife, rent on top of that – the man's wardrobe reflects his poor decisions.

'He's an insurance adjuster, just like he says he is. No trouble with the law,' he tells me. 'I tried to get hold of him to see if I could help him with anything, but he hasn't returned my call.'

'Alrighty then. Thanks.'

'That girl who's staying with you – who is she?' He moves further into the office and sinks into the chair on the other side of my desk.

'Daughter of a friend.'

'How long's she staying?'

'How is that any of your business?'

'Just making conversation.' He shrugs. 'You guys want to go to the ball game tonight?'

'Don't you have kids of your own to take to baseball games?'

'Spontaneity isn't part of the custody agreement.'

He seems lonely and I want nothing to do with that. But I don't have anything better to do and Lizzie must be getting bored.

'Okay,' I tell him.

He picks us up at six-thirty. He looks more comfortable in his jeans than he does in his work clothes. The ballpark on the northwest side of town is home to the Rangers' farm team, the Caprock Caballeros. The weather is fine, with a comfortable breeze and a few fluffy clouds in the sky. Everybody in the crowd is happy to be here. Seating

< 74 >

is general and we claim seats on the tenth row overlooking the third base line.

For once, Lizzie left her cell phone behind. She's thrilled to have an evening out. She skips instead of walks. She swings her ponytail, smiles, and pretends to be uncomplicated. She sticks close to Joe's side, at first shy about touching, but soon growing bolder so that her every breathy word is accompanied by a light stroke on his arm or thigh. She monopolizes his attention, giggling and asking questions, using a baby voice. The way she latches on to him communicates clearly that here is a girl with no male influence in her life. He brings it up when she's gone off to buy a hot dog.

'That little girl has problems.'

'Or she wants you to think she does.'

'So is her dad not around or what?'

'He died.'

'Little girls without fathers often have issues.'

'Or not.'

'I'm just saying.'

'You're just saying what?'

'Look, I'm a cop and I've seen things. There are a lot of sickos out there who prey on needy girls. A girl this desperate for male attention – well, it's just a matter of time until she finds it. She doesn't have a clue about real life or what some men are capable of.'

'Is she making you uncomfortable?'

'She's not dishing out anything I can't handle – but she's all over me in a way that's just not healthy. Where's her mother?'

'Italy.'

'The kid should be in counseling.'

'Leave it alone.' Lizzie's issues are not my concern and they're certainly not his.

< 75 >

And now we're irritated with each other, a situation that Lizzie intuits and exploits. Sitting on the other side of Joe, she begs him to explain the play-by-play. She asks what the statistics mean, why the umpire sweeps the plate, why the first baseman stands so far from the base. At one point I even hear her asking where the organist is.

Later, when Joe drops us off, he barely slows so we can hop out.

'I mean it!' he hollers at me as he drives away.

'That was fun,' Lizzie says. 'He bought me a hot dog, a Coke, a pretzel, and some peanuts. It was fun being able to just toss the peanut shells anywhere.'

Lizzie has found someone to buy her lunch two days in a row, and now she's listing an inventory of food that was purchased for her throughout the entire evening. Does she base her self-worth on people buying her food? Is this normal? Does Joe have a point? Lizzie is nothing to me. I would just as soon never have seen her again. But here she is, following me around, staying in my apartment. Is it fair to the world to allow a child to flourish wrongly?

Later, after she's gone to sleep, her phone emits a text ding. I cross the loft and take a look at the message.

Slumber party tomorrow at Mary's. When are you coming home?

And once more I'm flushed with anger at Nicole. Summers can be so fun when you're twelve, but here Lizzie is, far away from her friends and their slumber party, with only me and a bunch of old people for company.

My phone rings at midnight. It's Roxy.

'Middle of the night, Roxy Lynn.'

'Humboldt showed up here ten minutes ago and I killed him, just like I did Raymond.'

'I'll be there in half an hour.'

< 76 >

All There Is To It

Some people deserve to die, but they don't. And some deserve to live, and they die instead. I'm not shocked that Roxy Lynn killed the obnoxious man from Las Vegas. Death doesn't shock me anymore, but it's starting to inconvenience me.

'I didn't see this one coming,' Roxy says, reconfirming what I didn't want to know in the first place – that Raymond's demise was deliberate.

'Have you done this for your whole life – just taken the lives of people who cross you or don't behave the way you think they should?'

Though it's generally known that Roxy was once so quick to anger that she ran over her husband, up until a few days ago I saw her as a sensible and harmless old lady. She sells used band instruments. She bakes casseroles when one of the other vendors is sick. She dresses carefully, styles her pink hair daily, and refreshes her lipstick every hour. And though she's shorter than she used to be, she's energetic in a way that inspires middle-aged people to say they want to be as sharp as she is when they're her age.

Arthur Humboldt's body is splayed in the rectangle of light that slants from the kitchen window. Unlike Raymond, with the neat little hole in the forehead, Humboldt died a messy death. He took a bullet in the chest and

< 77 >

bled profusely. The front of his shirt is soaked in sticky red and the weedy dirt surrounding him is damp and stained a rich brown. His face is too young to belong to a dead man. Raymond's death didn't ruffle me because he was old, old, old. But this guy was only in his fifties. The lines fanning from the corners of his eyes are from laughter.

'A man doesn't want to get shot, he ought not to go peeking into an old lady's back windows in the middle of the night.'

'I'm going to want that gun back,' I tell her. 'I don't care for these interrupted nights.'

'What'd you tell the girl?'

'She was asleep. I didn't tell her anything.' Honestly, until just now, I'd completely forgotten about Lizzie.

'That's irresponsible of you. She's going to wake up and find you gone. Poor child, in an unfamiliar place. And it's spooky, too, on top of all those cold empty floors with that upstairs door leading to a dark alley.'

'You got a plan here?'

'At first I figured, well, he came looking for Raymond, so I'll just help him find him. But then I thought, I didn't have a relationship with this moron and I don't really want him planted in my backyard for all eternity. So what I'm thinking is Ransom Quarry.'

The old quarry is at least an hour away. About a quarter-mile into the posted area is a deep hole in the earth filled with dark water and surrounded by steep walls. I bet this won't be the first time it's on the receiving end of a dead body.

'You can't just dump him. You'll have to weigh him down or he'll surface.'

'We'll lock him in his car and roll it right over the edge.'

'Okay.'

< 78 >

'I want you to follow me out there and give me a ride home.'

'Why didn't you call Sherman and the other guys?'

'Last time I asked them for help, they charged me.'

'You paid them?'

'I asked them to do a favor as friends, and they wanted money.'

'How much?'

'A hundred apiece. Anyway, tonight I only need one person.'

They thought to ask for payment, but it never occurred to me. A hundred is a reasonable token, a compensation to secure their silence.

'You're paying me the same this time, then.'

After shooting me a dirty look, she bends over, sticks her hand in Humboldt's front pocket, and extracts a set of keys. She hands them to me and I go around to the front of the house to fetch Humboldt's Ford. The interior is dark and fetid, reminding me how he hawked a loogie in my parking lot. On the driver's seat is a key hooked to a plastic disc. I flip it over and, adjusting it in the beam of moonlight, read Lone Star 49. A motel room key. I didn't know any hotel in the world still used actual keys. I stuff it in my front jeans pocket.

I bump to a stop right beside his body and, working together, Roxy and I stuff him into the back seat. When we're done we both have blood and dirt on our hands, so we go into the kitchen and wash in the kitchen sink. The Beretta's on the table. It looks harmless, like a toy. I grab it, check that the safety's on and, when I get to my car, zip it into the center compartment of my purse.

Driving Humboldt's Taurus at the slowest speed possible, Roxy leads me over back roads I didn't know existed. Our two sets of headlights cut across the plains, disturbing

< 79 >

the nocturnal world of coyotes and owls. By the time she signals a turn to the quarry, I've fallen into a dull stupor in which meaningless thoughts float through my mind – how interesting it would be to visit a place where frogs live in trees, why vampires and werewolves have become so popular, the way my ears have been itching lately.

The odd thing about this abandoned mine is that while there are NO ENTRY and DANGER! signs posted along the fence every hundred feet or so, there's no gate to block the way, only a cattle guard. We drive right in. The road is poorly maintained, full of deep ruts, and our sluggish progression becomes even slower. I'm not happy about bringing my car in here; I fear I'm damaging my undercarriage. A rodent scurries through the beam of my headlights – a rat, I think. When we come to a stop at the edge of the pit, Roxy wants to transfer the body from the back to the driver's seat, but I see no purpose in it.

'To make it look like he drove in there himself by accident,' she says.

'But he's been shot. If and when he's found, cause of death will be obvious.'

'Not at first glance.'

'At second glance, though.'

'This is the way to do it.'

We prop him behind the steering wheel. I reach in and put the car in neutral. She locks and closes the doors. Taking up positions at the rear, we dig in, position our shoulders, and roll it forward. When the front wheels go over, the frame catches. We lift the bumper and the car simply falls over the edge. We rush to watch as it flips gracefully and splashes, roof-first, into the dark water.

'That's all there is to it, then,' Roxy says.

I drive her home, then head back to town.

< 80 >

The Typewriter Conspiracy

It's three a.m. and the building is a hive of quiet activity. Several familiar cars are parked in front and light spills out. Instead of circling around to the back the way I normally would, I turn into the front lot and pull up right next to Carly's VW. Abe's outside, leaning against the wall.

'What're you guys doing?' I ask, approaching him. I'm spiritually weary. Why does there always have to be something going on with these people?

'Just a little joke.' He's dressed all in black and the few white hairs on top of his head poke straight up.

The joke's on Sylvia, and it's more about them teaching her a lesson than playing a joke. At least ten vendors are working silently, taking the typewriters she stole from Pard's and distributing them throughout the other concessions. This is why Barry wanted the code and key card.

I weave my way through them without comment, heading toward the interior stairs. The light is on in the apartment and Lizzie is awake in bed, reading her book.

'They're downstairs moving typewriters around,' she tells me.

'I saw.'

'Where've you been?'

'Driving around the countryside.'

< 81 >

'Mom hasn't called. She said she would when she got there.' For Nicole promises are easy to make and easy to forget.

'If a plane crashed we'd have heard about it. I guess you must be enjoying that book.'

'I'm learning stuff.'

'Like what?'

'Like two people don't have to like each other to have sex. And no doesn't mean no.'

'Turn the light out.'

After she goes to sleep, I transfer the pistol from my purse to the safe.

In the morning people who usually don't show up until noon are through the door before ten. Their angry anticipation of Sylvia's arrival smells of sulfur and burned hair. It drifts through the building, adding its noxious blend to the moldy fug. Thriving on the emotional upheaval, Lizzie's eyes glitter as she pops into the office.

'The woman in the booth next to Laurence's wants to buy me a bicycle,' she tells me. She's wearing repeat clothes – same shorts as yesterday, same top as two days ago. I hate doing my own laundry, so it's a sure bet I'm not thrilled about being responsible for someone else's.

'Why would she want to do that?'

'She wants me to make deliveries for her. She said I had to ask you first.'

The booth next to Laurence's belongs to Sue, a grandmother several times over. Though Sue's shelves are laden with decorative breakables – porcelain, china, crystal, figurines – the inescapable truth is, she's a drug dealer.

'I don't think it's a good idea,' I say.

'Why? Don't you want me to get fresh air and exercise? It was your idea for me to work and earn money.' Here

< 82 >

comes the pout. This isn't about earning money, it's about someone buying something for her.

'You don't know your way around Caprock.' It's a weak excuse. Also, do I really care that this child who's not mine would be riding a bike around town exchanging pills for money and money for pills?

'Please, please, please.' She wrings her hands and pleads with her eyes – the same behavior that always got her whatever she wanted from Don.

'Take over doing the laundry and I'll say yes to the bike.'

'Thank you!' She skips from the office, ponytail swinging.

'Make her get you a helmet, too,' I call after her.

Every vendor is waiting to see Sylvia brought low. Janet, returned from attending the birth of her first great-grandchild, waves baby pictures and tells of a labor that lasted two days. The only person who's been left out of all the activity is our new vendor, Audrey, who shows up in my office looking puzzled.

'Hey, Audrey, how goes the recycled urn business?'

'Everybody got at least one of the typewriters except me,' she says sadly.

'You haven't been here long enough to be included in their revenge conspiracies,' I tell her.

'But I'm a friend of Genevieve's and she's been here for years. Shouldn't that count for something?'

'Doesn't look like it.'

Defeated, she slumps away.

I follow her out. When she goes downstairs, I go up.

I approach Marlina and Carly, who are huddled at Carly's counter.

'I've got a question,' I say. Pleased that I would come to them, they straighten and look helpful. 'Most times when a

< 83 >

man loses his wife or falls ill, you women can't wait to help out. But you haven't helped Laurence. Why?'

They share a look and shift their eyes.

'Come on. Laurence is one of the nicest men to have ever lived. There's got to be a reason.' It's unusual for me to have to coax. Usually they can't wait to tell me what's what.

'Laurence never could see anybody but Lydia,' Carly says.

'Also, he's made it known that when he dies the contents of his booth are to go to his brother.'

Ah. In Laurence there are no possibilities. There are almost thirty single women in the building, but he's not interested in replacing his wife. And he's leaving all his Christmas stuff to his brother, an affront to the grasping nature of every woman here. And extending the topic further – I bet that, other than talking about it, he's taken no step at all toward legally clarifying that he wants his brother to take over his booth when he dies.

'On to another thing, then,' I tell them. 'Full disclosure – Ken and I opened the box Pard kept in Mom's safe, and all that was in it was some old paperwork. Absolutely nothing of value. Spread the word.'

I tell them to have a good morning and wander down the stairs to see if Sylvia's come in yet. Taking the round-about route along the back and up the left aisle, I see Roxy in discussion with Abe who, I assume, is explaining why an antique typewriter appeared in her booth during the night. She gives me a sour glare as I rub my thumb across my first two fingers, a subtle reminder that she owes me money.

I turn the corner in time to see Sylvia come through the front door. There's a collective inhalation as heads crane to see her reaction.

She limps in, clearly favoring her tricky hip, reminding

< 84 >

every witness of her frailty. Her oversized knuckles clutch her cane so tightly that they're white from the strain. With her head as high as her humped back will allow, and her sharp eyes flashing a sardonic gleam, she calls good morning to Kathryn, who's pretending to rearrange her cup-and-saucer sets.

She follows up with good mornings to Dee and Margaret. Then she enters her booth, progresses slowly around her desk, and takes her place in the regal chair. Before her sits a single typewriter, a basic black Woodstock. There is no acknowledgement that yesterday there were many and today there's only one.

Now what they're all going to want to know is, who warned her?

Everybody returns to their tasks.

< 85 >

Post Another Notice

In the afternoon Lizzie wheels a Huffy cruising bike into the office. It's a beauty – pale green with pink trim, a pink basket on the front, and white-walled tires. A matching helmet, hanging by its strap, swings from the handlebars.

Sue's great-grandchildren wear clothes plucked from the racks at Goodwill. The last time her youngest great-grandson was in the building, his glasses were held together by masking tape; and the sole of one of his shoes had come unglued, which made it flap and fold back under his foot every time he took a step. Also, when we take a collection for something, Sue always manages to be elsewhere.

Yet for a stranger she shells out a couple of hundred for a bicycle.

'Congratulations,' I tell Lizzie.

'I don't have a lock. Can I keep it in here?' Her eyes glow with the excitement that comes from gaining a new possession.

'Sure. What kind of deal did you work out with Sue? Is she paying you by the hour, or per delivery?'

'I don't know. The main thing is, I'm supposed to check with her first every morning to get her schedule for me before I get started doing something for somebody else.'

It becomes clear. They're competing over who gets Lizzie.

< 86 >

And Lizzie's going to love taking advantage. I wonder how she's going to get all her loot back to Dayton.

'What's your favorite booth?'

'Christmas.'

Her mention of Christmas makes me think of Laurence. He and I need to have a talk. After instructing Lizzie to prop the bike behind the door, I make my way to his booth. He's perched on a high stool behind his counter, humming 'Joy to the World' as his bloodshot eyes gaze at the morning paper through magnified lenses.

'Got a sec?' I ask.

'Always.' He closes the paper, removes his glasses, and gives me his attention.

'Pard's passing taught me a lesson.' When dealing with the seniors I've learned to use euphemisms for death – passing, crossing over, meeting St. Peter. 'It taught me that we need to be clear about what we want done with the material goods we leave behind.'

'Now, Jessie, you're way too young to be thinking about who gets what when you're gone.'

'I've heard that you want the contents of your booth to go to your brother.'

'That's the plan.'

'Do you have that documented? Does anybody here know how to contact him or where your paperwork is?'

'There's plenty of time to see to all that.' Does Laurence still see himself as a man in the middle of his life? How much time does he think is ahead of him?

'Yes, but until you take that first step, nothing gets done.' It would only take a few minutes to make it legal. He could file his will at his attorney's office, or, like I offered, he could leave it with me and I'd see to it. What's it going to take to make this happen? Am I going to have to make

< 87 >

the appointment and deliver him to the lawyer's office? Am I going to have to do that with every one of these folks?

'What's with you lately?' Now I've hurt his feelings. 'First you tell us we got to get rid of our carpets, then you change the locks on the place. And now you're pestering me about something that's none of your business.'

'You're right. It's absolutely none of my business.'

I walk away. I might as well just accept it. I am the caretaker of the stuff these people leave behind. My mother was, and now I am. The designated death arbiter. I'll have cards made.

The original compromise the vendors and I reached was that they had two weeks to find a buyer for Pard's guns or I was turning them over to the authorities. And the chief negotiator of that agreement was Will, whom I haven't seen in a few days.

Will's booth is upstairs in the middle of the north wall. Themed around Coca-Cola through the ages, it's one of our more popular booths. Red and white ad signs, gadgets, decorations, toys, and memorabilia are placed on shelves, hung on walls, and displayed under glass. The two twelve-tiered bookcases that mark his side boundaries hold every style and size of Coca-Cola bottle produced over the last hundred years.

Will's not a good housekeeper. Everything in his area is covered with a coat of grime. The rug is so faded and filthy I can't tell what color it's supposed to be. Gray? Beige?

Centered on the back wall is a painting Will claims is an original Norman Rockwell, *The Old Oaken Bucket,* commissioned by Coca-Cola in the early thirties. Picturing a boy, a happy dog, and a bucket of cold colas, it's listed as missing on the Coca-Cola website and would be worth – well, the Coke people don't say how much they'd pay, but

< 88 >

I'm sure it's more than Will's ever seen. And yet here it hangs, unauthenticated, and blending in with all the other dusty red and white inventory.

Not my business.

Across the aisle from Will's, Charlie is talking to two customers, sleeveless beefy men with tattoos. In addition to finding homes for cars of dubious background – Raymond's, for instance – Charlie buys and sells hubcaps and other automotive accessories; and what he's doing with this inventory in an antique mall is beyond me. A skinny guy with a gray ponytail, he's one of the few people in the building who actually seems to take pleasure in saying goodbye to his merchandise. His territory is marked by pegboard partitions that are covered with mounted shiny circles.

'Hey, Charlie,' I call. 'You seen Will lately?'

'Not since the meeting at Pard's booth a couple of days ago.'

I return to the office, look up Will's home number. He doesn't answer until the eighth ring.

'Hello?' His voice is weak and croaky. And before I can identify myself, he starts coughing.

'Will?' I ask, hollering to be heard over a cough that's so harsh and violent that I fear his ancient brittle ribs will fracture from the strain.

There's a clatter, a bang, and a moan. Then silence.

I end the call and punch in 911. Reciting his address as I hurry out of the building, I race to my car. I'll meet them there.

The 911 call brought all first responders. Two police cars, a fire truck, and an ambulance are parked in the street in front of Will's house, silent with red and blue lights flashing. The firemen mill by their truck; two police officers stand beside the scrawny shrub up by the house; and a

< 89 >

couple of medics are wheeling a gurney out through the front door.

I park on the opposite side of the street and march across, meeting the gurney at the back of the ambulance.

'What's going on? How is he?' I look down at Will, who's looking pretty rough. He's got a gash above his brow and a bruise on his cheek – and when elderlies bump themselves the bruise isn't a polite muted blue, it's a glaring spread of magenta. An oxygen mask covers the lower part of his face and a drip has been inserted at the crook of his elbow. Seeing me, he reaches up with a shaky hand and pulls the mask from his mouth.

'You gave me two weeks.' He's talking about the guns.

'I sure did.'

'Now you're going to have to give me a little longer.' He pegs me with a bad-tempered squint, daring me to give a sick old man a hard time. I accept the dare.

'You want to go back on our deal because you're feeling puny?'

'Ma'am, you can talk to him at the hospital.' The EMS attendant replaces and adjusts the oxygen mask.

'What's wrong with him?' I ask.

'Not for me to say.'

She doesn't have to say. Pneumonia. So he's got a few days in the hospital on oxygen and antibiotics.

'Take care,' I tell him as they slide him into the ambulance. 'We'll be by in a while to see how you're doing.' By we I mean someone else.

'I mean it,' he growls. 'I'm going to need an extension.'

'No special treatment. Also, I'm removing that ratty old rug.' I can be quarrelsome, too.

This is the third time in the last year that one of the vendors has fallen seriously ill, each incident accompanied

< 90 >

by the full drama – the collapse, the ambulance, the hospital stay, the lengthy recovery. I haven't done a serious calculation, but I'd estimate that eighty percent of the vendors live alone. Children moved away and spouses died and homes that once held many now hold only one.

Back at the office I write this announcement:

> Concessionaires –
>
> Will is ill and has been taken to the Methodist Hospital. I'm sure visitors will be appreciated. If you'd like to donate money for flowers, please put it in the collection box.
>
> Also, it seems like a good idea to instigate a buddy system in which two people contact one another on a daily basis – watching out for each other is just good sense.

This isn't the first time I've suggested that the vendors check on one another, but the few times I've mentioned it, they've interpreted my concern as interference. The notion that one of them might tumble or trip, be unable to rise, lie on the cold bathroom floor for days, and die – well, it's a potential scenario that fills me with helplessness. But for some reason they don't seem at all concerned, as though this is a situation that simply would not, could not, occur.

I pin the notice on the bulletin board right next to the one I posted a few days ago. The collection box is centered on the table beneath the bulletin board. In a few hours it'll be stuffed with ones.

< 91 >

Cleaning Up

At the end of the day the collection box at the front of the building has twenty-seven dollars in it, which will perfectly cover a bouquet and delivery from flowerland.com. After ordering the flowers I walk around the building guilting seniors until I get three who say they'll stop by the hospital on their way home.

After that, mentally preparing myself to get dirty, I stop by Will's booth. The entrance to his area is marked by an opening between two trestle tables. As is the case with most of the carpet remnants throughout the building, it's held in place by shelving and tables, with wide tape at the periphery to smooth the edges. The tape along the front of Will's area is cracked and curling. I get down on my hands and knees and peel it back, breaking two fingernails and getting sticky filthy residue on my fingers. Then, crawling further into the booth, I lift the legs of the tables and pull the carpet from under them.

When I notice Charlie watching from his booth, I call him over to lift the corners of the bookshelves. He's reluctant.

'This is an invasion of Will's property,' he says.

'It's policy.'

'It's theft.'

'Look at how nasty this carpet is, Charlie. It's no wonder Will's in the hospital with a respiratory infection.'

< 92 >

There's no arguing with that. With a sigh, he lifts the corners of all the cases and shelves a couple of inches so I can pull the carpet out. I find six dead cockroaches and more dried-out spiders than I can count. It was too fusty for even the insects to survive. Charlie flees the scene as soon as I free the last foul corner.

I fold the rug over itself, wrestle it out through the gap between the two tables, and spread it in the aisle. It's about sixteen by eighteen. As I roll it up dust flies in all directions, coating my clothes and hair and attacking my eyes and sinuses. Grasping one end of the cylinder, I drag it all the way to the back of the building and out the back door to the alley. Vendors look on and mutter.

What I find at the dumpster makes me mad. In the residential areas of Caprock there's a garbage pick-up service. People leave their wheeled bins out by the street a couple of times a week and trucks come by, tip the bins into a gigantic hold, and haul the household trash away. But the city doesn't collect the garbage of commercial enterprises. Businesses like mine hire private waste disposal companies and they don't come cheap. Yet when the people who live in neighborhoods have items that're too bulky to fit in their bins they dump their junk in or around my container.

Right now there's a small couch sitting next to my dumpster. It's an ugly shade of rust; and one of the front legs is missing, causing it to lean forward and to the side. Because it's beside the container and not in it, I'll have to call Dumpster Kings and pay extra to have them come and haul it away. And I'll have to do it quickly, before one of the vendors sees it and decides it's worth something. I prop the top of the rolled carpet on the ledge of the dumpster, lift the bottom of the roll, and dump it over and in. Then I go in and call the collection people.

< 93 >

I itch all over.

After my shower I take Lizzie to the grocery store for our usual graze at the salad bar and whatever protein we're in the mood for. We decide on hamburger patties and she picks up a single bun from the bakery section so she can make a burger. At the deli counter she asks for a single slice of cheese.

'The woman I'm staying with doesn't have a refrigerator,' is the excuse she gives when the woman behind the counter seems dismayed by a request for so small an amount. Lizzie adds this unsolicited information: 'I'm only allowed to buy a tomato if I promise to eat the whole thing, not just a slice. And no mayonnaise or lettuce because they have to be refrigerated. And I don't ever get French fries, either, because she doesn't even have a stove, or any appliance, really.'

The deli woman gives me a look saying she thinks I'm a monster, which is exactly what Lizzie was aiming for.

'You keep that up, it could backfire,' I tell her after she collects her cheese. 'Some person's going to feel so sorry for you they're going to turn me in to Child Welfare. You'll be placed in foster care. The world will lose track of you. Your mother won't know how to find you when she gets back.'

'Like she'd even bother to look.'

After dinner we gather our laundry and shove it into garbage bags. I'll show Lizzie how to wash, dry, and fold this one time, just to make sure she's got the hang of it, then for the rest of the summer she's on her own.

As I'm stuffing the jeans I wore last night into the bag, my fingers knock against something solid in one of the pockets. It's Humboldt's room key. I forgot about it. It might be wise to get over to the Lone Star and get his things out of there. I drop the key into the side pocket of my purse and later, after Lizzie's settled across from the washer with

< 94 >

her novel, I tell her I'm running an errand and I'll be back in less than an hour.

Constructed of cinder blocks and painted mint green, the flat-roofed Lone Star is a relic from the fifties. Located on Caprock Boulevard, it's infamous due to a murder that took place there over sixty years ago — a woman, thirty-something, found nude and stabbed through the heart in one of the rooms, never identified. In a place as uneventful and forthright as Caprock, a violent unsolved murder can keep speculation churning for decades.

I pull up in front of room forty-nine, which is at the back of the single-story L-shaped building. On the other side of the chain fence that marks the hotel boundary is a weedy lot with bits of trash caught in the weeds. At the far corner of the vacant lot is a quick-stop store.

I lock the car, approach the door, unlock it, and step inside. It's pretty much what I expect — a stuffy room with an unzipped duffle bag atop a cigarette-scarred desk, and a few personal items strewn around. Underwear and a pair of socks are on the chair in the corner, and I toss them into the duffle. Then I go into the bathroom and grab his tooth-brush, toothpaste, and razor, and stuff them into the duffle. I have another look around the room. There's a photo of a young woman and a child propped on the nightstand, and his phone's on the charger next to it. Just as I'm reaching to pick up the picture, the phone starts playing a tune.

My feelings are mixed. Arthur Humboldt didn't make a good impression. But even men who are gross and annoy-ing have people who love them. Acting on impulse, I slide my finger along the answer display, but I don't speak; I just hold the phone to my ear.

'Daddy?' The woman sounds young. 'Have you and Raymond picked up the collection yet?'

< 95 >

My heart is pounding like she's standing right here in the room.

'Daddy? Are you there?'

I disconnect, turn the phone off, grab the photo and charger, and toss the items into the duffle with the rest of his stuff. I place the key on the desk and leave the door unlocked when I leave. After dropping the bag in the trunk, I slide behind the wheel, reverse, and drive away.

I should never have answered that call.

I call Roxy, who sounds groggy.

'Did I wake you up?' I ask. 'It's barely eight o'clock.'

'I lost sleep last night. I'm old. I need my shut-eye.'

'Do you know where Raymond was staying? I'm assuming a hotel. Maybe we should clear out his things.'

'I thought about that, but the fact is, I just don't know.'

'It'll draw attention when he never goes back and his things are still there.'

'Arthur Humboldt was staying somewhere, too, but there's just no way to know where.'

'The Lone Star. I already took care of it.'

'Wouldn't it be great if, when a person dies, all the stuff they leave behind just disappears? Just *poof* and it's gone.'

Ironic, considering how she and the other vendors have been fighting over a dead man's stuff.

'Come on, Roxy, think. The man's been coming back to town for years. There had to be some regular place he stayed.'

'It's not like we exchanged pleasantries. Under a rock as far as I know.'

'Did you think to go through his pockets or his car?'

'There wasn't anything in his car. His pockets? No, I didn't look.'

'I'll be out around ten. You go ahead and get your rest now because you're going to need your energy.'

< 96 >

Later, after the laundry's been sorted and Lizzie's settled in front of the television, I fetch Humboldt's duffle bag from the car and dump its contents on my bed. Clothes, toiletries, the phone, and the framed picture. I study the photo. The boy in the picture isn't healthy. No hair, exhausted eyes, thin gray face. I'd estimate seven years old. He sits in his mother's lap and she has her arms around him. The woman is in her twenties, pretty, with thick dark hair and warm brown eyes. Her smile is forced. She and her son have the same features – pointed chin, thin lips, and short turned-up noses that, come to think of it, are similar in shape to Humboldt's nose.

The conclusion is obvious. This is the woman on the phone, daughter of Humboldt; and the child is her son. And, while I thought Humboldt was a pest, he was a man caring enough to carry a photo of loved ones with him when he traveled. She called him to check on him. This is not a man to disappear without someone noticing he's gone.

I pack it all back in the bag and place the bag on the floor of the safe, right below the shelf that holds Pard's cash.

< 97 >

Another Night at Roxy's

In a year the soil where we buried Raymond will have settled, but right now it's a distinct hump on the otherwise flat landscape. Roxy and I step out her back door and walk toward the area beside the fence posts.

'Was he right-handed or left?' I ask.

'Right.'

'You should get something planted out here, ground-cover of some kind.'

'Maybe.'

My feet sink slightly as I cross the recently disturbed area. It's ten-thirty, but it feels like much later. The breeze sweeps gently toward the east at about five miles an hour. The stars are bright and far away, making me think of my husband and babies at their inaccessible distance. Do souls move into vacant stars when they no longer have bodies to inhabit? I think one of the religions believes this to be true. But no. Dead is dead.

I slide the shovel in, lever it, lift it out, and toss the load to the side. Push, lever, lift, toss. It's not long before I'm sweating. The exercise feels good.

'I'm there,' I tell her when the shovel thumps against the body.

'Here.' She bends toward me, offering the box cutter, but I'm fed up. This grizzly chore doesn't belong to me.

< 98 >

'No. Your mess, you clean it up.'

I climb out of the hole and help her into it. She plants one palm on the ground to brace herself as she crouches and wields the blade toward the dirt-coated tarp. But, as she's already pointed out several times this evening, she's old. Her fingers are so misshapen by arthritis that she can't even achieve a firm grip, which makes me wonder how she held and aimed the Beretta. She's simply unable to get the job done.

'Okay, I'll do it,' I tell her, disgusted.

'I'm willing.' Her watery eyes convey an apology. 'I'm just not up to it.'

I help her out, then clamber back in. She gives me the box cutter. I study the shape of the form that I've uncovered. It looks like my estimate about the location of his front pants pocket was right on. I bend at the waist and slash through the layers of tough plastic sheeting. A current carries the foul odor straight up my nose. I squat and try to insert my hand through the opening, but the cut's too small. So I grip the gash at one end and saw at the other, lengthening it. The stink is unimaginable – sweet and rotten sewage mixed with sharp gas that stings my eyes. I stand and, stretching as far away as I can without actually stepping out of the hole, take several cleansing breaths. Then, taking an inhalation that'll last, I stoop once more to complete the task. Slipping my hand through the opening, I work my fingers into the pocket of the baggy pants of the corpse.

Success.

I extract the key card and leap out of there.

'That couldn't have been easier,' Roxy says.

I study my right hand, the offender of nature, the white lump at the end of my arm. Beneath the fabric the texture of his flesh had been squishy and slack. My fingers will

< 99 >

remember the feel of it forever. My hand will never be the same.

The number scrawled on the inside of the key card envelope is 126, and it's from the Best Western on the interstate. I stick the small folder in my pocket and start filling the hole. Roxy stands to the side and smokes a cigarette while I scoop the dirt in and pat it all over with the back of the shovel. When the area's smooth once again, she drops her cigarette butt on the mound and presses her heel into it, marking the site with a child-sized contemptuous footprint. We head back toward the house.

'I'm charging a hundred for this, too,' I tell her.

She sighs.

We go into her kitchen and while I wash my hands, she goes to fetch the money.

'This little mission tonight was your idea, and it was completely unnecessary,' she says as she flattens two hundred-dollar bills beside the sink. 'So I'm meeting your demand under protest.'

'I'm trying to keep you out of prison.'

'You'd go to prison, too.'

'You think I care?'

'You're too young to have given up this way. Everybody suffers. What made you think you'd live a pain-free life?'

'What could I possibly have done to make you think I'm open to a personal conversation?'

'If Alicia were here, she'd tell you to pick yourself up and get on with your life.'

'My mother's dead. And getting on with my life is what I'm doing. I get up in the morning. I accomplish things during the day. I eat and sleep. I deal with all you loony people.'

'But you won't allow yourself to be happy.'

< 100 >

'I used to be one kind of person. Now I'm another.'

I snatch my two hundred and stomp out the back door. I've left without drying my hands.

In the car the steamy odor of my fury mingles with the nasty stench of a three-day corpse. Everybody knows they don't talk to me about what happened. They know it. And yet that's exactly what she did. Who does she think she is, making comments about me like she knows anything about anything? She has no right to an opinion about how I get through the days. She has no right to lecture. She has no right to talk to me about my mother. So what if I'm not the ray of sunshine I used to be?

I'm angry all the way home. And dammit, I meant to talk to her about the phone call I answered on Humboldt's cell. The woman mentioned a collection. What collection? I intended to ask, but Roxy made me so mad I couldn't bear to be near her anymore. When I pull into my regular parking place in the alley I'm still angry, too angry to go inside and go to bed.

So what I do instead is I enter through the downstairs back door and make my way to Roxy's booth. The musical instruments mounted on her walls cast whimsical shadows – the bell of the saxophone is an opening blossom; the guitar is a woman of grace and dignity; the trombone is a giant's paperclip. Lots of people find pleasure and comfort in music. Maybe I was too quick to accept Lizzie's rejection of the idea that she learn to play an instrument.

The carpet in Roxy's booth is the same as the carpet in many of the other booths – worn, grimy, smelly. Just like with Will's, I rip up the tape, lift the corners of all the fixtures (some are quite heavy, but I manage) and yank the ratty fabric out from under. I haul it to the alley and shove it up and in.

< 101 >

Then I go back into the building and lock up from inside.

Before I go upstairs I take another detour to Roxy's. Circling around behind the counter, I start a search through the deep drawers that run along the bottom. She keeps the smaller instruments in here. The four spacious drawers hold mostly woodwinds – piccolos, flutes, clarinets, oboes – there are a few coronet cases, too. I rifle through the flutes. I don't know what to look for in a flute, so I just choose the one with the nicest-looking case. I'll sign Lizzie up for lessons tomorrow. And great, now she's got me spending money on her.

Roxy'll know I took it, but I really don't care.

< 102 >

Raymond's Stuff

Sue, our octogenarian supplier of drugs, is overweight and slow-moving, a calculating old woman who glowers from behind her glasses with cynical eyes. In her twenties and thirties she had six freckled broad-nosed kids; and each of those kids grew up and had several more freckled broad-nosed kids, who also eventually reproduced. Every once in a while she has no choice but to take care of a great-grandchild or two, and on those days the whole building feels like it's been taken over by a rowdy horde. She retired from nursing over twenty years ago and she's been operating her booth ever since. Though mainly her shelves hold breakable collectibles like cream pitchers, crystal bowls, and cup-and-saucer sets, she's taken on some items that don't belong – a couple of spinning wheels of mysterious origins, an antique Singer, and the bellow sets she lifted from Pard's. Oh, and newly arrived, a very old Remington typewriter.

When I stop by her booth there are a couple of young women exclaiming over one of Sue's most impressive acquisitions – a complete set of Spode, Eden pattern, excellent condition.

'It's beautiful,' one says. 'You think it's dishwasher safe?'

'I would never risk it,' the other says.

Seated in her comfortable chair in the front corner, Sue

< 103 >

doesn't bother to address their query. They'll never buy it, anyway. She's got it priced at twice what it's worth.

'Got a sec?' I ask.

Sue offers a regal nod. I remain on the outside of her area, addressing her from the opposite side of the counter.

'Lizzie said you've got her biking around town this afternoon.'

'Yeah.' She's wary.

'I know you've got this deal worked out with her, and I'm good with that. I just want to remind you that there are places in town that you don't want to be sending a twelve-year-old girl by herself.' Mostly Caprock is a safe place, but, like most mid-sized towns, it's got its dubious neighborhoods.

She squints at me, evaluating subtext, looking for something to take offence over. Though no insult was intended, she manages to find one.

'You think I'm going to put a child in danger? You think I just arrived here yesterday, that I'm unaware of what goes on in this town where I was born and raised and have lived for over eighty years?'

'As long as we're on the same page.' I expected her to take umbrage. Indignation's what keeps these people alive.

'And another thing.' She's pleased to have me in front of her, happy to tell me what I'm doing wrong. 'You've got to quit pushing this buddy plan of yours. I don't want anybody calling me every day, checking on me, and putting their nose in my business. And I don't want the responsibility of calling anybody else.'

'I can't force you. I thought it seemed like a good idea.'

'What I want to know is who died and left you in charge?'

The pain is swift and piercing. I react physically, cringing

< 104 >

away from Sue, who has the decency to look ashamed. It's one of those humorous things people say, but she needs to think before she talks.

'My mother, that's who. My mother died and left me in charge.' I give her a mean look before stomping away.

Lizzie was thrilled with the flute, another item to add to her summer collection. Whether she learns to play it or not remains to be seen, though I've set her up with a private lesson tomorrow morning. Right now, she's working in Carly's booth. I climb the stairs to the second floor. Pard's area is now completely empty. Even his tables and shelving have been claimed and hauled out. Across from Pard's, it looks like Lizzie's availability has inspired Carly to do some cleaning. All the better-quality jewelry has been moved out of the display cases, the black velvet lining lies in a crumpled heap outside the counter, and Carly's going after the cubby beneath the glass with a handheld vacuum cleaner.

Sitting at a card table inside the booth, Lizzie seems content as she dips chains into a jar of jewelry cleaner and straightens them on a towel to dry. I wave my hands above my head to get her attention.

'I'm running a quick errand,' I holler over the roar of the vacuum. 'Back in an hour.'

Unlike the Lone Star, which is in the seedy part of town, the Best Western is a two-story brick rectangle located on the highway that runs through the busy commercial section. And it has interior access only, so there's no way I can drive right up to the hotel room door like I did at the Lone Star. Hoping to avoid interaction, I'm reluctant to enter through the lobby. So I drive around the building looking for a less conspicuous way in. All I find is a single metal door at the back of the building. Pulling to a stop, I check my surroundings. Mine's the only car back here. A

< 105 >

high brick wall marks the three-sided perimeter. A dumpster sits in the furthest corner.

I get out of the car and approach the door. Three signs are posted – NO ENTRY, LOCKED AT ALL TIMES, and STAFF ENTRANCE ONLY. They really don't want people coming in through this back entrance. Because security seems to be an issue, I scan the eaves and fence for cameras, but I don't see any.

An electric lock is mounted right above the knob. I push the key card into the slot and pull it out; the green light blinks, and I slip through the doorway. So much for their safety measures.

The interior carries the combined scents of air freshener and scorched linens. To the right, through a fire door, is a staircase. Stretching straight before me is a single narrow hallway. The assault of orange and green carpet, peach walls, and low ceiling makes me feel claustrophobic. There is no sound or movement. The number on the nearest door is 156. Hunching like an enemy spy, I slink up the corridor to 126, dip the key, and enter with ease.

Not quite as large as the room at the Lone Star, but similarly furnished, Raymond's room is overly warm. The curtain on the other side of the bed is closed, making the room dark. I flick the switch on the wall and the lamp on the desk comes on. The floor in front of the door is littered with notices. I pick one up. It's a request that he stop by the front desk.

The bed's made up and his clothes are spread neatly across his closed suitcase, which rests on the luggage rack. I fold the clothes in half and, opening the suitcase, place them inside. There's an iPad on the desk, and I toss that, along with its charger, on top of the clothes. I take a few seconds to ponder the anomaly. The eighty-somethings in

< 106 >

my sphere wouldn't have a clue what to do with an iPad; they'd call their lack of technical know-how virtuous, and it'd make them proud.

There appear to be no other personal possessions in this room, and so I go into the bathroom. The bathroom's tight. There's no counter space – only a bathtub, sink, and toilet. Above the tub is a window of fogged glass. Several pill bottles are lined up along the back ledge of the sink. A toothbrush and toothpaste are on the toilet tank.

The knock on the door makes me jump. Adrenalin surges. Leaping back out into the main room, I look around in a panic. No place to hide. No excuse for being here that makes sense.

A woman's voice identifies, 'Hotel management.'

Grabbing the iPad, I dash back into the bathroom and close the door.

She's speaking as she enters the main room, her high-pitched voice easily penetrating the insubstantial bathroom door.

'He prepaid for five days,' she says, 'and when that came and went, and it was obvious he was still staying here, we tried to contact him. After a few days the maid reported that the bed wasn't being slept in.'

'And how long's it been since anyone's seen him?' It's Joe! What the hell?

I can fit through the window.

'Oh, I couldn't give you an accurate time on that – '

Stepping into the tub, I release the latch on the window and push it upward.

'So where are his – '

I set the iPad on the sill, clamber through the opening, reach in, grab the iPad, and close the window.

Then I run.

< 107 >

Uncomfortable Revelation

'I'm not here to tattle,' Carly tells me from the doorway.

'And yet here you are. What are you not going to tattle about?'

'That little girl you got staying with you is a thief.'

'What did she take?' I'm not even going to bother denying it. Carly knows her inventory.

'A cameo locket, French vintage.' Vintage is code for looks antique, but it isn't.

'I'll get it back to you.'

'When?'

'In the next day or two.'

'You're not going to apologize for bringing a delinquent into the building?'

'Nope.'

'You might want to rethink your attitude.'

She disappears from the doorway.

I don't know why I grabbed Raymond's iPad. I went to get his stuff, and when that became impossible, I guess I felt like I had to carry something out of there. I didn't think to grab the charger, though. Luckily, it's seventy-percent charged, and it's not password protected, which is typical of an old guy. Propped on the desk before me, it offers a horrifying revelation.

In the picture gallery are photos of Humboldt with his

< 108 >

daughter and his sick grandson. Also, there are photos of Raymond with Humboldt's daughter and child. The little boy is pale and thin, but his grin is heroic. And there's one of Raymond and Humboldt together, their arms wrapped across each other's shoulders in manly affection. And while it's true that Raymond's wrinkled and lined features gave his countenance in death a belligerent and discontented aspect, in the photos those same features are lifted in merriment. His eyes twinkle with warmth.

Three generations of adults circled around a sick child, that's what I'm looking at. A small family and a family friend. People who care for each other.

Is it possible I believed the wrong person? A drunk, Roxy called him, and a cheat. She told stories of his petty vandalism and threats. Sparks of bitter hatred snap all around her when she says his name. And I never once considered the source – an old lady whose prejudices and vices are all that motivate her to get up each day, a woman whose initial reaction to every mildly inconvenient situation, throughout her entire life, has been nasty and violent. Hell, she ran over her first husband.

There's a tap on the door. I look up to find Joe leaning in.

'Hey.' He moves into the office and settles into the chair on the other side of the desk. 'I'm going to have to disturb you for a minute.'

'What's going on?' I slide the iPad into the center drawer.

'You know that guy who was in here looking for the husband of one of your vendors?'

'Ex-husband.'

'He hasn't been seen for several days.'

'The insurance adjuster?'

'No, the guy he was looking for – the ex-husband. His clothes and a suitcase are in his hotel room, but the bed

< 109 >

hasn't been slept in for a while. His medications and toiletries are still in the bathroom. I've been trying to get hold of the other one, the insurance guy, but he still hasn't returned my calls. Did he mention where he was staying?'

'All I knew about him was what was on his card, and I gave that to you.'

'Which one of the old ladies out there is the wife? I'm going to want to talk to her.' He stands and gives me a look, obviously expecting me to escort him to Roxy's booth, which I do.

'Oh. She's not here,' I tell him when we arrive to find her area unoccupied.

On the other side of the partition, Abe hums to himself as he picks through coins.

'Hey, Abe,' I call to him. 'Do you know where Roxy is?'

'She hasn't come in yet, that's all I know.'

Joe and I turn toward the exit.

'What's with all the typewriters?' Joe asks.

'I don't know. They got hold of some typewriters. Collecting stuff is what they do.'

'You know we searched Pard's house, right?'

'Yeah, you told me. Looking for firearms that don't exist.'

'And what we found instead were old typewriters.'

'Do you really want to make an issue of this?'

'No, I guess not.' We come to a stop at the front door. He reaches into his pocket, pulls out a couple of his cards, and hands them to me. 'Have the wife give me a call.'

'Ex-wife.'

'How's the girl? She behaving?'

'Not really.'

With a disapproving smirk, he walks out the door. I watch as he ambles toward the department clunker, his unattractive suit hiking up in back and hanging shapelessly from his shoulders.

< 110 >

As I'm turning to go back to the office, Kathryn calls to me from her booth.

'What's up?' I ask, approaching her counter.

'I want to lodge a formal complaint about what I'm forced to look at day-in and day-out.'

I follow her gaze to the eyesore on the other side of Paramount. The debris that was pushed to the center of the lot by the bulldozers remains as they left it – an unstable mountain of bricks, concrete, and drywall that's twenty feet high at its center. People explore the foothills, poking around for things of value. She's right; it's not a stimulating scene, but there are several such piles of rubble in town.

'Seriously? You called me over to gripe about the view?'

'It's a mess and a danger and nobody's doing anything about it.'

'Do you really believe I have a say in city cleanup? Or do you just love to complain?'

'I also want to talk about Dee. She's not herself today. Her mind's been skipping around a lot lately. She's been getting confused. But today she can't seem to shake it.'

A jerk of her head indicates the neighboring booth. I glance over. Dee is unmoving and staring vacantly at the front door, which is unusual because Dee is the type who's always bustling around, rearranging, folding and fussing over her inventory.

'Who in this building isn't confused? The other day I came across Estelle all the way up on the second floor looking for the restroom. She's been in this building for twenty-five years and she forgot what floor the restroom was on.'

'That's not the kind of confused I mean. Everybody gets disoriented now and then.'

With a good-bye tap on Kathryn's counter, I turn toward

< 111 >

Dee. Dee's collection tends toward the feminine. As a rule, she changes her presentation daily, but today her center display is the same as it's been all week. Her gaze grows fretful at my approach.

'Hi, Dee,' I say. 'How're you today?'

'Hi, Alicia.' She thinks I'm my mother. 'I'm waiting for my mom to come get me. I need to get home.'

'Your mom?' Her mother's been dead for half a century.

'She'll be here any minute. It's time for me to go.'

Damn it. 'You want me to go call her?'

'Yes, please. Tell her I'm ready to come home.' Her eyes have become the eyes of a child, incongruous in their nest of creases, sags, and liver spots.

I return to the office.

I've met Dee's daughter, Tina, a time or two. She and her husband both retired a couple of years ago and now they spend their days traveling around the country in their RV. Thankfully, she's in town. Her voice is clipped and breathy when she answers her phone.

'Tina? It's Jessica, from the antique mall.'

'Oh. Hi.'

'Your mother seems confused.'

'Is she talking about her mom again?'

'Yes.'

'Oh, well, she just has these spells now and then. Listen, I'm on my way out of town. We're going to the Grand Canyon – second time this year.'

'Tina, your mother seems to think someone is coming to pick her up.'

'She'll snap out of it. You just watch. In a few minutes she'll go on out to her car and drive herself home.'

'But what if she – '

'I've got to go. Take care.' And she ends the call.

< 112 >

It's true that Dee usually drives herself. I return to the front of the building and see that yes, her ancient Volvo is out front. Taking this as confirmation that Tina knows what she's talking about, I return to Dee's booth. She's still fixated on the front door, but her accelerated blinking and shallow breathing signal impending panic. This doesn't look like a woman who's going to get in a car and drive anywhere.

'You want me to run you home?' I ask.

'My mother's expecting me. She'll worry if I don't get home soon.'

'Let me grab my purse and keys and we'll go.'

On the way back to the office I come across Lizzie wheeling her bike in through the back door.

'Hey,' I say. 'I'm fixing to run one of the vendors home – want to come?'

'Sure.' She stores the bicycle in my office and runs off to check in with Sue while I look up Dee's address.

On some days my priorities change every five minutes.

< 113 >

Disaster House

Fifteen minutes later I pull up in front of Dee's house.

'Here you are,' I tell her.

She's been restless on the drive over, wringing her hands, clutching at her seat belt, and sighing. By contrast, Lizzie, in the back seat, has been quiet, thoughtfully gazing out the window.

'What is this place?' Dee peers at the pleasant brick house with the tall elm in the yard and the screened-in porch. 'Where have you taken me? You said you'd take me home.'

'This is your home. You live here.'

'This isn't where I live. I live with my mommy and daddy on Monroe Street.'

'Let's go in. There're some things inside I think you'll recognize.'

Dee has been a collector all her life. When I was a kid I came over here once with Mom. I must have been about nine – and what's odd is that I don't remember much about my day-to-day life when I was that age, but I remember everything about that visit. Dee's house was like a museum, full of intricately carved furniture and faded photographs. She gave me cookies and led me around the house, telling me the history of every possession – where she got it, how much it cost, who she was with at the time. She seemed old to me then, and that was twenty-odd years ago.

< 114 >

In order to get her to enter her own home, I have to promise that her mother is waiting inside. She hangs on to my arm as we walk through the door. Ponytail swinging, Lizzie bounces in behind us and heads straight to the cushioned rocker in the living room. She sinks into it and immediately starts a back-and-forth motion.

'Whose house is this?' Dee asks.

I'm hoping her possessions will remind her who she is. I walk her through, telling her as much about the items as I can remember – the oak sideboard her great-grandmother brought from North Carolina, the doilies and runners tatted by ancestors dead for over a hundred years, the colorful pair of fans she bought at an outdoor market in Hong Kong sixty years ago. Every item is coated with dust.

My goal is the wall in the hallway where her family pictures are arranged. I guide her through the living room and turn the light on as we enter the hallway. The pictures still hang, positioned as I remember them, fair and chubby faces going almost as far back as the Civil War.

'Here.' I point to the first photo. 'Do you remember who this is?' Two rosy-cheeked kids stare out. Dee was probably about five, her brother maybe three.

'Me and my brother, Alvin.'

'And who's this?'

'My mother.' The woman in the picture is about sixty, heavy, with tight gray curls. 'But she's old. How did she get so old?'

'Hon, you're old. You're an old woman now.' I guide her to the bathroom, turn her toward the mirror. 'Look at yourself.'

This is probably the wrong way to go about this, but I can't think of anything else to do.

'What happened to me? I'm really old.' She presses her

< 115 >

liver-spotted hands to her crepe cheeks. 'This can't be me. But it is.'

'Yes.'

'And you say I live here? In this house? And all these nice things belong to me? But if I'm this old – where is my mother? Oh, no – where is my mother?'

She meets her own gaze in the mirror and her drooping lower lids flood as she faces the death of her mother all over again, only this time as a child. *This isn't my situation to handle.*

'Come back to the front room. I'll make you a snack.'

Dazed and miserable, she allows me to lead her back out to the living room. Motioning Lizzie to move to the couch, I settle Dee in the rocker. A few minutes later, when I return with a sandwich and a glass of milk, the television is on, and Dee seems calm. I set the plate with the sandwich on the small table beside her chair.

'Dee, we're going now.' I write my number on a piece of paper and, placing it next to the sandwich, say, 'Call if you need me.'

Eyes fastened to the screen, she doesn't acknowledge my words or the sandwich. We leave her there. I've got her daughter on the phone before I reach the car.

'Listen, Tina.' I'm furious and I sound it. 'Turn that stupid RV around, get back here, and take care of your mother. Dementia doesn't get better; it only gets worse, and you're all she has.' This time I'm the one to end the call.

'Dee for dementia,' Lizzie says as she snaps her seat belt in place.

Taking the highway home, I impulsively get off at the Errol Street exit. I take the first right and pull to a stop. Across the street is a pink brick house that lacks charm and balance. It's the Disaster House, dubbed so because fifteen

< 116 >

years ago, three times during a six-month period, the house was crashed into by cars getting off the highway. It had never happened before, and it hasn't happened since. There was no explanation for it. The angle at the exit ramp wasn't hazardous; the curve was negligible, the access road was broad, and the boundaries were clearly marked. Also, there was no construction in the area and the weather conditions on all three occasions were fair.

People talked about it for years.

'Why are we here?' Lizzie asks.

'Just taking a breather. The house is a local landmark.'

I tell her the story of the three inexplicable crashes.

'Why are you telling me about something that happened so long ago?'

'Because it's still talked about. In a place as uneventful as Caprock, people don't forget unusual things. You're going to have to give the locket back to Carly.'

'Okay.' I'd expected some sort of prevarication.

'Why did you take it?'

'Laurence gave me a Santa Claus. Marlina gave me a little dish with flowers on it. Sylvia gave me a lacy shawl. Emily and Thomas gave me a magazine from the year I was born.'

'And Carly didn't give you anything.'

'Yeah.'

'Shouldn't giving you something be her decision?'

'People should give people things to remember them by.'

The only thing I saved of my time as a wife and mother was a photo album, which I couldn't bear to look at; so I locked it in a safe deposit box at Dayton First National figuring that when I was ready for it, it'd be there. All the other things – Don's clothes, books, gadgets; the girls' clothes, toys, baby beds – I donated to the charity resale shop. And during this purge, I gave no thought to Lizzie at all.

< 117 >

'I finished the book I was reading,' she says, 'and I traded it to Emily for another one.'

'Don't you have a list of required reading for the summer?'

'Should you have left her there like that?' She's talking about Dee.

'I did the best I could.'

'We need to stop by the music store and buy that beginner's flute book.'

I buy her the book, a music stand, and a small electric metronome; and that evening, instead of watching TV or fiddling with her phone, she spends a couple of hours figuring out how to produce a sound on her flute, and learning which fingers to press down to make notes. After a while she goes to bed, turns on her reading light, and pulls out a book. The cover is similar to that of the last book she read – except on this one, the woman's improbable curls are brown, and the chiseled man wears a Stetson. She's exchanged pirate sex for cowboy sex.

Later, after Lizzie's turned out her light, I'm unable to settle. I get out of bed, trudge down the outside stairs to my car, and drive over to Dee's. A gigantic RV takes up the entire driveway. Light spills from the windows of the house and, inside, shadows shift. I go home and go to sleep. The next morning when I unlock the front door, I look out to see that Dee's Volvo is gone from the parking lot.

< 118 >

A Not-so-Pretty Truth

'We need to talk.' Sherman stands in my doorway. His hair is combed and creases have been ironed into the sleeves of his plaid shirt. He wants something from me and I'm pretty sure it has to do with Pard's firearm collection.

'You taking over now that Will's out of circulation?'

'All he needed was more time, but you wouldn't give it to him.'

'If everything came to a halt every time one of you got sick, nothing'd ever get done around here.'

'Will and I want to offer a compromise. You want to unload 'em, and the two of us are willing to buy 'em, so let's do that, and then we can all relax about it.'

If this happens, those guns'll never go anywhere. They'll be buried in a drawer or a box, just like when Pard had them. And I'll be stuck with the task of getting rid of them again in a couple of years.

'I want them out of the building.'

'We'll see.'

'You're going to buy out the other vendors?'

'That's the plan. It'll take the burden from you and give us time to find the right deal. It's a win-win.' The right deal. Hah. Once they have possession, they'll never let them go.

'How much are you offering?'

'Fifteen hundred.' He wants them so badly he's willing to pay more than they're worth.

< 119 >

'Tell me the truth, here. Are you going to sell them and get them out of the building – or are you going to hang on to them?'

His only answer is a shrug. As far as he's concerned, if he and Will buy them, what they do with them is none of my business.

'Let me ask around,' I say, 'see how the others feel about it.'

'It's the only option.'

'No, it's really not.'

My response irritates him and he shuffles away in a huff.

Sherman doesn't have a box in the safe, but Will does. I've been meaning to have a look at what's in there ever since he went to the hospital, but there've been distractions. I close the door and, crossing to the safe, open it and rearrange the boxes in order to dig out Will's, which is at the bottom of the stack.

Will's box holds a couple of hundred dollars and the paperwork and corresponding padlock combinations to three units at Big Boy, a storage facility on Adams. That he'd have a storage unit isn't surprising. Many of the vendors have more inventory than fits into their booths, so they store the excess off-site, though most have only one unit, not three.

Keeping the sheet with the combinations out, I lock and replace Will's box, grab the iPad, and head toward Roxy's booth. Several people are gathered outside her counter, with Sherman in the center. He's already making his case. When they see me coming they slink away as though I'm the principal and they're up to something naughty. Roxy puffs up her chest and starts accusing me while I'm still ten feet away.

'That girl's up there right now, taking a lesson on a flute that isn't hers.' Her angry energy causes her bridge to click

< 120 >

with every word. 'You didn't even try to be sneaky about it. And you owe me for that carpet.'

'You have no right, no right, to accuse me of doing something wrong.' I put the iPad on her counter, pull up the picture of Raymond with the boy, and say, 'Take a look at this.'

'What kind of hellish technology am I looking at?' She places her glasses on her nose and leans in.

'It's an iPad.'

Impatient and angry, she taps the counter with a bright red fingernail as she views the pictures.

'This is all I was able to get out of Raymond's hotel room,' I tell her. 'I got interrupted before I could get the rest. Now the police have decided it's a suspicious disappearance, and they're going to want to question you.'

I hold out Joe's card, which she ignores. So I place it on the counter.

'Who is this child with Raymond? Why are you showing me this?'

'It's Humboldt's grandson, obviously a very sick little boy. And Humboldt's daughter called, asking if he and Raymond had picked up the collection yet.'

Roxy pulls in her chin when I mention a collection.

'What collection, Roxy Lynn?'

She releases a rough sigh, as though my demanding the truth is an act of cruelty.

'Tell me.' I move into her space. Taller, healthier, and generations younger, I'm disgusted that I'm forced to use intimidating tactics on this feeble undersized eighty-something.

'Okay, okay, look. After the divorce, when Raymond left town, he left his baseball card collection with me. For safe-keeping, he said.'

< 121 >

'And he wanted it back.'

'After that long a time it wasn't his anymore.'

'I'm assuming they're valuable.'

'Some are, most aren't. Valuable's not the point.'

'Then what is?'

'I wasn't his storage facility. You can't just come asking to take something back after thirty years.'

'I've got a whole story in my head,' I tell her. 'Raymond was trying to get his baseball cards to show them to his friend's sick, possibly dying, grandson. Humboldt came to pick up the cards with Raymond and take them back to Las Vegas. I don't know why they came to town separately, but for whatever reason, they were going to meet up here. Mainly, what I see are two dead men who were trying to do a good deed, and there's someone waiting for them in Las Vegas.'

'Raymond never did a good deed in his life, and don't you say otherwise.'

'Do you know what it's called when you kill someone who doesn't need killing?'

Stubborn, she presses her lips together and squints with malicious eyes.

'Murder, Roxy, it's called murder. And you've dragged me into it. And Ken and Sherman and Barry. What's your next move? How are you going to fix this?'

It's a ridiculous question. There's no way anyone can undo what's been done. Giving a final tap to Joe's card on the counter, I take the iPad, and leave her standing there.

Back in my office, I mull. What's the penalty for accessory to murder? Years in prison, that much I know.

Lizzie bounces in. The T-shirt she's wearing is a bit tight across the chest and I notice that her nipples have enlarged and taken on definition. They were flat yesterday. Does it

< 122 >

happen that fast? Looks like we're going bra-shopping this afternoon.

Her new flute teacher follows at a more sedate pace. I'd expected a girl, but the band director sent a boy, Bryan. With the clear skin and blond hair of a Scandinavian, Bryan's a pretty seventeen-year-old. Each of his cheeks displays a bright red slash, an extreme blush that, I suppose, is the curse of being so fair-skinned.

'Hey. How'd it go?'

'Fine.' Plopping into the chair, Lizzie radiates enthusiasm. 'Did you know it takes more air to play the flute than any other wind instrument?'

I send an inquiring look to Bryan, but he looks away. He charges twenty dollars for half an hour. I take a twenty from my purse and hold it out to him.

'You got a minute?' he asks, accepting payment and stuffing it in his front pocket.

'Sure.'

Instead of speaking, he sends a silent head signal toward Lizzie. Oh. He wants to speak to me privately.

'Lizzie,' I say, 'Emily wanted to see you.'

She hops up, and with a 'see you later' skips out the door.

'I think it'd be better if you found someone else,' he tells me as soon as she's out of hearing range. Everything about him says he's spooked – his flushed face, his wary posture, the way he clutches his flute case to his chest for protection.

'Okay. Was something wrong?'

'No.' He's looking everywhere except at me. 'I think, you know, she might be better off with a girl. I have a friend I can recommend.'

What the hell? He hands me a piece of paper with the name and number of his friend, then he leaves.

< 123 >

Three Units

Lizzie fiddles with her seat belt, pulling it out and releasing it so that it snaps against her abdomen. She has the thrilling misconception that we're going to Victoria's Secret, that her new bra will be trimmed in red lace, and that it'll transform her small knots into sexy boobs. She'll be disappointed when I take her to JC Penney's and buy her a couple of plain whites. I've thought about it and decided that whatever went wrong in the flute lesson, it's not my concern. So I surprise myself when I bring it up.

'Bryan isn't going to be able to teach you after all.'

'Why? I liked him. I thought he liked me.' She looks hurt. Real or pretend, I can't tell.

'Did something happen?'

'I don't know.'

'Sure you do. Was there a point during the lesson when things got weird or awkward?'

'When I asked him if he'd had sex.' She knows what's appropriate and what's not. Did she deliberately set out to sabotage the lesson?

'If you didn't want to learn to play the flute, all you had to do was say so.'

'No. I like the flute and I like him.'

'Then why did you ask him something you knew was off-bounds?'

< 124 >

'How am I supposed to know things if I don't ask?'

'Why the hell do you need to know if your flute teacher's had sex or not?'

'It's an interesting thing to know.'

I suppose it is. There's the inevitable disappointed sigh when I turn into the Penney's parking lot.

'Is this the only store you know?' she asks.

'You're getting a training bra,' I tell her as I park the car, 'not runway lingerie.' We get out and head toward the entrance.

'Why hasn't Mom called?' She's thinking that her mother should be the one with her when she gets her first bra. I agree.

'She will.'

I buy her three bras at seventeen dollars each. Soft, lightly padded, and white, they go on over her head like sports bras. She wears one out of the store. As soon as we're in the shimmering heat of the parking lot she starts complaining that it's hot and itchy. Welcome to the world of women, little girl. I find myself wondering how Don would feel about his daughter growing boobs and thinking about sex. Don wasn't sentimental. If he were alive and I told him I'd just taken Lizzie bra-shopping, he'd most likely shrug and ask what was for dinner.

'Why are we going here?' Lizzie asks a few minutes later when I turn into the Big Boy lot.

The compound is made up of several paved and narrow alleyways that run between rows of units fronted by garage doors that are locked at the bottom. The units belonging to Will are 213, 214, and 215. I park in front of them and, taking the sheet with the lock combinations, get out of the car. Lizzie gets out and follows me to 213.

'These three belong to Will.'

< 125 >

'The guy in the hospital?'

'Yeah.'

'Does he know you're doing this?'

'Hasn't got a clue.'

Squatting, I spin in the combination, free the lock, and raise the door.

The odor of stale tobacco, offensive and sharp, smacks us in the face. Shelves line the three sides of the small area and a two-sided shelf in the center reaches to the ceiling. The shelves are loaded with hookah pipes – three deep, fifteen rows from side to side on five shelving units, each unit having four shelves. Ancient and modern; brass, porcelain, and plastic; fat bases and narrow; colorful and plain. Feminine in shape, hoses extend from the rounded midsections like gracile arms.

'What are these?'

'Hookah pipes.'

'What are they for? How do they work?'

'They're Middle Eastern, or Mediterranean. How in the world did he come by these in this part of the world? There must be several hundred of them.'

All I can conclude is that he bought the whole collection from a single source.

I decide to leave the door open and let it air out. I don't know what he's thinking. If he wants to sell these things in my building, he'll have to sterilize every one of them. The place smells foul enough as it is. I can't have this horrendous odor added to the mix. We move on to the next door.

The same shelves and interior, only this unit is filled with – and honest to God, I can't think why – two-gallon and four-gallon jars holding biological oddities. Preserved in what I assume is formaldehyde, there are several two-headed

< 126 >

kittens, multiple rats sharing a single tail, a piglet with a leg growing out of its back, organs sprouting repulsive growths of thick black hair.

A five-by-five sign leans against the back shelf. Once colorful, now faded, the block letters of the roadside billboard spell out NATURE'S MISTAKES! SEE THEM NOW! NEXT EXIT!

'What the hell is he thinking?' And now I can't help but rant. 'What happens to all this useless crap when he dies? Does the world really need it? Is it really worth saving? Dirty water pipes and grotesque abnormalities. What's the attraction? A hundred bucks per unit per month – why?'

Beside me, Lizzie sighs, saying, 'I really liked Bryan.'

The third unit holds two collections – ball caps on one side, colorful boxes on the other.

The caps are fitted one into the other, forming trains that stretch from the back of the unit to the front, taking up four shelves, with three rows per shelves. I do a mental calculation. There are over a thousand baseball caps.

The colorful boxes that look like board games are actually jigsaw puzzles. Six boxes per stack, ten stacks per shelf, eight shelves. Approximately four hundred and sixty puzzles.

'Want a jigsaw puzzle?' I ask Lizzie.

'Sure.' She starts going through the nearest stack. 'Hey, some of these are pretty old.'

'I imagine they are.'

In the future, when Will has been planted in the marble orchard – his favorite euphemism for death – the vendors will fight over these puzzles. Estelle will claim they should be hers because she has toys, and puzzles are a kind of toy; and Ken'll say they'll fit just as well into his stock, because he's strong in paper media and isn't that what jigsaw puzzles are? Also, they'll all want something from

< 127 >

the hookah collection. Hell, some of them'll even want the freak show.

'Do you think he'll come back if I apologize?' We're back to Bryan.

'Honestly? I think he's right and you'll be better off with a girl teacher. And don't ask her if she's a virgin.'

She chooses a thousand-piece dogs-playing-cards puzzle. I close and lock all three units and we return to the car just as my phone rings. It's Joe.

'Hey,' I say. 'Did Roxy ever get hold of you? I told her to call.'

'We've got a meeting lined up in half an hour. She asked if it'd be alright if you were there and I said that was fine. She sounds really old.'

'I told you.'

'So your office, thirty minutes?'

Half an hour later, Lizzie, thrilled to see Joe, leaps at him, knocking him sideways a few steps. He rolls his eyes at me as she takes his hand and leans into him, wanting a hug. All she gets is a wary pat on the shoulder.

'Don't you have some errands to run for Sue?' I ask her.

'I want to stay here with Joe,' she says.

Roxy appears in the doorway. Leaning on a cane and listing to one side, her usually straight back is hunched. She looks tiny, frail, and helpless. So that's the way she's going to play it.

'Okay, I'm here.' A wheezy tremor has been added to her repertoire of elderly affectations. 'What's this about? Something to do with Raymond, you said?' Limping in, relying heavily on the cane, she lowers herself into the chair slowly, as if she fears her bones might snap.

'Joe'll still be here in a while,' I tell Lizzie. 'But right now he needs to talk to Roxy Lynn.'

< 128 >

'Promise?' Still hanging on to Joe's hand, she looks at him with pleading eyes.

'He promises he'll try,' I answer for him.

With a final squeeze of his hand and another soulful look, she skips out to the floor. Joe gives me a glare before he moves toward Roxy. He offers her his hand, introducing himself. Slow to respond, she searches his face fearfully before raising her trembling fingers to accept his shake. The formality out of the way, Joe shifts to my desk, perches his backside on the front edge, and faces her. I take a stance behind her, placing my hands on her shoulders, playing the part of supportive friend.

'You were married to Raymond Verney?' Reacting to the scene we've set for him, Joe speaks slowly, keeping his voice neutral and his body position unthreatening.

'A long time ago. Why?'

'There's concern that he might be missing. When was the last time you saw him?'

'Missing? Oh, he'll turn up. Just like a bad penny. He wasn't reliable when I was married to him, and I doubt he's reliable now.'

'When did you see him last?' he asks again.

'He was always moody. I never knew what he was going to do next. You say he's gone missing?'

'Has he been in touch with you?'

'Married for ten years, divorced for thirty.'

'Mrs. Verney, has your ex-husband, Raymond Verney, been in touch with you? Have you seen him recently?'

'If he's in town he might drop by my booth. Do you want me to have him call you if he stops by?'

'Yes, if you see him. But, that's my question – have you seen him? Has he dropped by?'

'I think I'd remember if I'd seen him.' She cranes her

< 129 >

neck around, looking up at me with feigned confusion. 'Has he dropped by? Did he come by and I don't remember? Sometimes I forget things.'

'I don't know,' I tell her. 'I haven't heard that he's been here.'

'He might come by if he's in town. Is he in town?'

Joe's had enough. He straightens off the desk.

'Okay, that's all I need for right now. Thanks for your time, ma'am.' He turns to me, asking, 'Walk me out?'

Giving Roxy a kindly shoulder squeeze – for his benefit, not because I'm feeling kindly – I leave the office with him.

'That old woman belongs in a home,' he says. 'Are they all this way? How do you stand it?'

'She forgets things and sometimes she comes up with things that can't be true. People tend to lose focus when they get old. But they like showing up here and hanging out in their areas with their stuff. They socialize and bicker. It's good for them.'

'She shed no light and now I'm back to square one.'

'What'll you do now?'

'Wait and see.'

When I get back to the office Roxy's still there.

'Well?' Back to her usual perky self, she wears a smug grin, like she's expecting praise for her performance.

'Do you think we're bonding over this?' I give her my nastiest glare until she gets up and stalks out the door.

< 130 >

A Mother's Call

My phone rings: Caller Unknown.

'Hello?'

'Is she settling in?' It's Nicole. There's noise in the background – laughter and the festive clash of silverware and dishes. She continues, not giving me a chance to answer, 'I'm borrowing a friend's phone because mine doesn't work here. Everything's going great. I'm getting so much work done and the class mentor is encouraging and so very perceptive. It's glorious, practically a holy experience, to be surrounded by people who share my vision and understand my work. I feel so alive. Inspiration is everywhere. I mean it. I can't look in any direction without feeling compelled to create.'

'She keeps her phone with her all the time hoping you'll call. So why are you calling me instead of her?'

'Because for the first time in years I feel free and she'll just make me feel guilty.'

'Guilt is what happens when you pretend to be free and you aren't. You have a daughter who needs you. Dumping her here was cruel and irresponsible.'

'See – now you're guilting me.'

'When are you coming back? Give me an exact date.'

'I finish here the last week of July. But there's been buzz about an extension. And one of the other artists has a house outside Naples.' I do not like the sound of this at all.

< 131 >

'So? You have a house in Dayton.'

'I've got to go.' And she terminates the call.

Don's first wife. I tolerated her crap for five years and I shouldn't have to deal with her now that he's dead. I hope with all my heart that something horrible happens to her.

Lizzie pops in and begins to extricate her bicycle from behind the door.

'I'm picking something up for Sue,' she says.

'Did you return that locket to Carly?'

'I'll do it later.'

'Do it today. And apologize.'

'Okay.' She wheels the bike from the office, ponytail swinging, off to pick up some Xanax or Oxycodone from one of Sue's many relatives.

'Wear your helmet,' I call after her.

This isn't the time to tell her about Nicole's call. I might never tell her. It sounds like Nicole wants to stay away longer than she originally planned. Is she giving me her daughter? Does she think that because I lost my own little girls, I'll accept this precocious pre-teen, the thieving first child of my dead husband, as a replacement? No. She doesn't think that because she never thinks; rather, she acts impulsively and in her own interests without considering anyone else, even her own child. She doesn't know what I know – that children are precious and fragile and they can be lost forever because of something as commonplace and insignificant as a sneeze behind the steering wheel.

I wander down to the basement to get a look at the new tenant's booth. Audrey Persons and her urns have taken over the section between Estelle's antique toys and Ken's comic books and superhero memorabilia. It's interesting to see that she's done something different with her display – staircase shelving instead of straight-up bookcases, which

< 132 >

allows for better viewing. Sitting in a foldout lawn chair in the open area in front of her booth, Audrey directs a teenage boy in the placement of the last of the urns.

'Hey, Audrey. How's it going?'

'Almost finished,' she says as her helper sighs. 'This is my grandson, Pete. Pete, say hello to the boss.'

'Landlady, not boss,' I correct. The kid and I nod to each other. To Audrey, I say, 'Talk me through your inventory.'

Struggling to stand, pushing herself up using the chair's arms (arthritic knees) she makes a sweeping gesture toward the higher back shelves.

'Those that Pete's arranging now are the oldest and most valuable,' she tells me. 'Some of them actually contain remains from as far back as eighty years ago.'

Oh. I thought she'd be selling urns for future use, not ones that are currently being used.

'Cremation wasn't so much of a tradition back then,' she continues, 'so these are very rare. And you might've even heard of some of these folks.'

She lists the people whose remains are for sale – Elwood Marrs, mayor of Caprock from 1942-1954, died 1963; Karin Bay, notorious madam of the Swales Saloon, died 1950; Chaney Wright, of the Wright Ranch, died 1986. The list stretches to about twenty people who influenced the tri-state area during the last century.

'How much are you asking for these remains?'

'It depends. Like Edith Pace, who actually had speaking lines in three beach movies in the sixties – for her I'm asking four hundred. For Harold Hardy, who founded the school board down in Chester, two hundred. And the ones intended for recycling are from one to one-fifty.'

Four hundred dollars for the ashes of a beach movie starlet. Audrey's going to be right at home here.

< 133 >

I wish her luck and head back upstairs.

Dee's booth is adjacent to the top of the stairs on the ground floor, and I see that Tina, Dee's daughter, has come in. She's sorting and folding, her motions similar to her mother's. Is Tina taking over her mother's booth? Or will she be closing it now that Dee can no longer keep it going?

'Hi, Tina.' I approach the booth. 'How's your mom?'

Tina continues her motion as though she hasn't heard. I speak louder.

'Tina – how's Dee?'

Once again, no response. She's giving me the silent treatment. Hostility stiffens her spine and makes her movements sharp and abrupt. She's mad at me? She's blaming me? What a baby.

There was a time when I was absurdly susceptible to the moods of others. I'd worry for weeks over someone else's foul mood, offering false cheer and apologies for things I had nothing to do with. And when someone's anger was directed at me, every shadow I cast would be the color of despair. These days I really don't give a damn. Leaving Tina to stew in her baseless antagonism, I return to the office, where I replace the sheet of paper with Will's combinations in his box.

For dinner that evening Lizzie and I split half a pre-cooked chicken and a container of coleslaw from the deli section. After we eat, Lizzie practices her flute for a while. She practices what she calls long tones – the notes sound airy, but a definite pitch comes through. She also tries to play a song that sounds vaguely like 'Three Blind Mice'. Then we dump the jigsaw puzzle on the table and fit pieces together. After that, Lizzie watches a fun and silly drama about high school girls, sending and receiving texts through the entire show – apparently it's popular with her and her

< 134 >

friends. Then she goes to bed and reads. She places her phone next to her pillow. She doesn't want to miss a call from her mother.

Exhausted, I climb into bed, turn my face toward the wall, and immediately sink into slumber. Three hours later I wake up and see that the light over Lizzie's bed is still shining. Thinking she fell asleep with it on, I start to get up to turn it off. But no, she's still awake and reading. I guess cowboy sex must be as gripping as pirate sex.

< 135 >

Respect

'Well?' Hovering in the doorway of my office, Sherman wants an answer about the guns. His eyes glint intensely from behind his thick lenses, like he's trying to influence me with his mind.

'Fifteen hundred and you get them out of the building.' I'm sticking to the deal.

'That might be a problem. We might need to store them on the premises for a while.'

'No.'

'Pard did.'

'That was a pre-existing arrangement. This time it's my say, and I want them out of here, and I don't want them available for rent anymore.'

'Then we need some extra days to find another place to store them. And once they're ours, we can do whatever we want with them.'

'You've got a week before I hand them over to the police.' There's one of them, though, that I won't be turning over.

'With Will in the hospital, we might need more time.'

'One week.'

He gives me a dirty look before shuffling from the office. Nobody seems to be getting along with anybody these days.

My phone rings. It's Joe.

'Hey, what's up?'

< 136 >

'A development. Arthur Humboldt has just been reported missing by his daughter.'

'The insurance agent from Las Vegas?'

'The one looking for Raymond Verney. According to the daughter, he was coming from his sister's in Oklahoma City, stopping here in Caprock to meet up with Verney, who'd come from Las Vegas. They were planning to pick up some old baseball cards from his ex-wife. I'm going to have to talk to her again.' I can hear his bewilderment. People don't usually go missing in Caprock.

'You saw what Roxy Lynn was like.'

'The daughter hasn't heard from him in a couple of days. She says she expected him back by now.' He pauses, as though waiting for me to respond in some way, which I don't do. After a few more seconds, he returns to the subject of Roxy. 'Is there a time of day when she's more lucid?'

'Not really.'

'Will you get ahold of me when she gets in?'

'Sure.'

We end the call. Pulling Raymond's iPad from the center drawer of my desk, I set it in front of me and open his email.

Three days ago he received a schedule of his usher duties for the next three months, sent by the sanctuary coordinator of St. John's Methodist Church.

There's also a schedule of his hours at a soup kitchen.

There's a thank-you-for-serving acknowledgement from a charity fun run.

I want to slap Roxy Lynn Verney so hard her face'll fly off.

Carly pops her head in. I tuck the iPad in the drawer.

'Hi,' I say. 'Did Lizzie return your locket?'

'I let her keep it.'

< 137 >

'What? Why?'

'She cried when she apologized. That poor little girl, she likes pretty things and she and her mother don't have much money.' She seems to think that's an acceptable excuse for stealing. 'Hey, Laurence's brother's in the building, if you want to meet him.'

'The brother he's going to leave his booth to?'

'You're going to want to write another one of your notices. Do us all a favor and resist the urge.'

She's made me curious. Carly and I leave the office. She heads upstairs and I take a right, toward Laurence's booth.

I've made a reasonable assumption that if Laurence's brother is going to inherit the Christmas collection, he must be younger than Laurence. I revise my notion as soon as I set eyes on him. There's a possibility he's younger – once a person goes beyond eighty-five or so, well, old is old. But he sure isn't in as good a shape as Laurence. On oxygen, in a wheelchair, missing the bottom part of one leg, so thin he's no more than coated bones – this guy could topple over dead any second. What is Laurence thinking?

'Jessica! Come in and meet my baby brother.' With a sweeping gesture, Laurence invites me into his booth. 'Renny, this is Jessica, the owner of the place.'

'Hello, Renny.' I bend over to shake his hand, which is trembling, misshapen, and covered with brown spots. 'It's good to meet you.'

He smiles at me from a mouth that holds six long teeth the color of ancient scrimshaw.

'Laurence's booth is one of the most popular in our building,' I tell him. 'Do you like Christmas as much as your brother does?'

'Yar, yar.' His head leans to one side, and he obviously has difficulty getting words out.

< 138 >

Carly's right. My first instinct is to run back to the office and pound out a notice about how silly it is to leave the contents of your booth to someone who's only going to live for a week after you're gone. Not my concern. Telling Renny that it's been a pleasure, wishing the two of them a good day, I walk away.

Roxy's with a customer. The contrast between her and the guy is noticeable – she's itty-bitty, wrinkled, and most likely carries the smell of cigarettes; but she's well-dressed in white pants and a pink floral blouse the same shade as her hair, and her eyes are bright and mean, like little birds' eyes. The guy, over six feet tall, is in his mid-twenties. He wears a torn and faded T-shirt, badly needs to do something less disastrous with his long thin hair, and possesses the dull eyes and slack forehead of someone who has few thoughts.

A case is open between them on the counter. Roxy holds a trumpet in her hands, turning it in all directions as she examines it. She'll buy it from him for fifty and price it at four hundred.

'Roxy,' I say as I pass, 'I need you to come see me when you've got a minute.'

She signals acknowledgement with a nod. The guy at her counter is putting out an odor that tells me it's been several days since he's bathed.

I hustle on by, heading toward the office. Fifteen minutes later Roxy steps in. She takes the chair and glares at me, still irritated by what I said to her yesterday.

'Joe called and he wants to talk to you again,' I tell her. 'Humboldt's daughter's filed a missing person's report on him. Joe knows about them wanting the baseball cards. So, two men gone missing in Caprock, and the only lead the cops have is you.'

< 139 >

'He can ask questions until the cows come home, for all the good it'll do him.'

'He's got a job to do.'

'I'll muddy his waters, but I'm going to want something from you in exchange.'

'What?' The audacity. Who does she think she is, to be making demands?

'Respect.' She's channeling Don Corleone who, come to think of it, was also a sociopath.

Exhausted from dealing with Roxy and her corresponding wreckage, I sigh, drop my head, close my eyes, and hold the position. There's a rustle and a creak as she shifts. Then, growing even more impatient, she clears her throat. I'm following trails in my mind, hoping to put some definition to this situation, wishing there was a way I could go back a week. If I had a do-over, I sure as hell wouldn't rent her that stupid Beretta. The truth is, there's nothing I'm willing to say that'll satisfy her. After a couple of minutes, giving up on my inner meanderings, I lift my head and once again give her my attention.

'Roxy, I know you live by a code that places high value on ownership and possessions – all of you do. But you killed two good men because of a baseball card collection. I've got lots of feelings about what you dragged me into, but respect isn't one of them.'

'Then you'd better find some. Arrange it with the cop. But I want you to change the way you're thinking about things.'

Turning, she walks toward the doorway and pauses there, as though she has something else to say; but then, with a grunt and a shake of her head, she continues on her way.

< 140 >

Share and Support

Joe calls again, asking if Roxy's arrived yet.

'Yeah, she's in the building. I was just fixing to call you.'

'Is she doing better?'

'Better than what? I told you yesterday – what you saw is pretty much all there is to her.'

'Did you know she did time?'

'Ran over her husband. Ancient history.'

'Is there a place where she'd be more comfortable? Would her home be better?'

Joe sitting at Roxy's kitchen table, looking out her back window, eyeing the freshly churned rise out by the leaning planks. Yeah, that's not going to happen.

'No, I think here is best.'

'Okay, be there in fifteen.' He disconnects.

Not wanting to hike to Roxy's booth again, I use the ancient intercom, which is something I hardly ever do because it tends to emit painful squeaks. Also, it alerts everyone in the building to things that are mostly none of their business.

'Roxy.' *Screeeek!* 'You're needed in the office in fifteen minutes.'

Joe shows up in ten, same awful suit, same arrogant assumption that what he's about to see and hear is the truth.

< 141 >

'Hey there, come on in,' I greet him, hoping to get this over with quickly. 'Roxy Lynn's on her way.'

'You never did tell me about the girl.' Bringing a hint of heat from outdoors, he relaxes into the chair, crosses ankle over knee. 'Who is she and why's she here?'

'Her mother wanted to go be artsy in Europe for the summer. Lizzie's basically been dumped here against her will.'

'And her father's dead?'

'Yes.'

'Her father was your husband?'

His face reflects all the appropriate emotions – concern, compassion, grief, empathy. I hate seeing this look. I hate when people offer condolences. What's really stupid is their belief that their sympathy will be appreciated or that it will make any difference at all to the texture of my impermeable grief.

'You need to change the subject.'

'Why didn't you tell me you lost your husband and children? Why didn't you correct me when I thought you were divorced?'

'Who gave you the right to study my life?'

'Did you think I wouldn't find out? I'm a detective. I detect.'

'Stop talking right now.'

'We've known each other since we were kids. We're friends. And friends talk to each other. They share and support.'

Share and support, words I've come to hate. How do you share something that's too agonizing to articulate? Why would you want to? And why seek or expect support from others who can't see beyond their own miserable stories?

Roxy appears in the doorway, cane in hand. She's changed her look since I saw her fifteen minutes ago. Pink

< 142 >

hair, which had been sprayed into a brittle helmet, is now fluffed out at the sides, Dagwood-style. Her blouse is buttoned crookedly and she's removed her bridge, leaving startling gaps between her teeth.

'You wanted me?' Leaning heavily on the cane, she creeps into the room like a shy second-grader.

'Roxy Lynn, you remember Detective Epps, from yesterday?'

Joe rises from the chair and turns to greet her.

'Yesterday?' She says the word as though yesterday is a new concept to her. The lack of the bridge gives her even more of a lisp, which enhances the impression of childishness. Clearly befuddled, she accepts his hand.

'Hi, Mrs. Verney.' He motions her to the chair and props his butt on the same corner of the desk he occupied last time he talked to her. Today, instead of standing behind her, I choose to remain in my chair behind the desk.

'You've talked to Detective Epps before, Roxy Lynn. Remember?' I address her as though she's frail and precious. I know my role in this farce.

'No. Sometimes I forget things.' She shakes her head slowly, keeping her eyes fixed on his face as she searches for familiarity. 'We've met?'

'Mrs. Verney, I need to ask you some questions about your husband.'

'Which one? I had two.'

'Raymond Verney.'

'Raymond? He lives in Las Vegas.'

'But he recently came to Caprock.'

'Did he?'

'Have you seen him?'

'We're divorced.' Her gaze seeks mine. 'How long have Raymond and I been divorced?'

< 143 >

'At least thirty years,' I tell her.

'Yes,' Joe says, 'but it's my understanding you were still in touch.'

'We didn't have children.'

'Have you spoken with Raymond Verney recently?'

'He lives in Las Vegas.'

'Do you know a man named Arthur Humboldt?'

'Who?'

'Arthur Humboldt. Did your husband ever speak of him?'

'Which husband?'

'Raymond.'

'Raymond? He's my ex-husband. Why are you asking about him?'

'Both Raymond and his friend, Arthur Humboldt, have gone missing.'

'Why are you here? Who are you? Why are you asking me about Raymond?' Her query is fretful, as though she's on the edge of tears.

'Now, Mrs. Verney, I just need to know a few things.'

She swallows, once again turns her mystified eyes toward me. I give a nod of encouragement.

'All I need to know, Mrs. Verney, is if you know anything about some baseball cards that belonged to Raymond Verney. He was going to contact you about them.'

'Raymond was going to contact me? I haven't seen Raymond in years. We're divorced.' Once again, she turns to me and asks, 'For how long?'

'Thirty years,' I tell her.

Joe's exasperation takes the form of a sigh. But he doesn't give up.

'Mrs. Verney, have you spoken to your ex-husband, Raymond Verney, in the last week?'

< 144 >

'I don't know. I don't think so. Have I?' She looks at me as though I hold the answer.

Reacting to her cue, Joe also turns and, over his shoulder, gives me an expectant look.

'How the hell would I know?' Now I'm the one who's exasperated. 'I just own the building. I don't keep track of their personal lives.'

Joe stands, thanks Roxy for her time and, same as he did yesterday, asks me to walk with him.

'Well?' I ask when we're standing by the front door.

'She was less coherent today than she was yesterday. How am I supposed to find out anything from someone who can't even remember what happened twenty-four hours ago?'

'What's your next step?'

'Do you know anything about any baseball cards?'

'Look at this place.' I make a gesture that encompasses the whole building. 'We've got a guy here who's got a collection of deformed animals and body parts preserved in formaldehyde. And a woman who's trying to unload used urns. There's too much useless stuff in the world. Baseball cards? Who gives a damn?'

'You and the kid want to get some pizza tonight?'

'Sure.' Lizzie will be thrilled.

'Meet you in back at seven.'

I watch as he saunters across the lot, gets in his car, and takes a right on to Paramount Boulevard. Then I rush back to the office. Roxy's gone. Good. I pull the iPad from the drawer and continue my search through Raymond's email. Specifically, I'd like to find a message from Arthur Humboldt's daughter. I don't know her name so I have to open and skim each one. And then I find it, sent and received a week ago:

< 145 >

> R – it was sweet of you to bring the balloons by the other day and to take time to read to Mark. Daddy says he's going to be meeting you in Caprock to give you moral support when you collect your baseball cards from your ex-wife. He called her a real piece of work. Mark's got a whole scenario playing in his head where the three of you pore over the cards and you and Daddy tell him all about the great players. Of course, when he imagines it, he's a hundred percent healthy and after you talk about the cards, the three of you go outside and play catch. I have faith that it's going to happen someday. Thanks, God bless, and we'll see you soon. M

I'm not gifted when it comes to technology, but I know there's such a thing as a remote IP address. It takes me an hour to figure it out, but I finally manage to get on with a server out of Dallas. I reply to M's email:

> M – Arthur and I are in Dallas visiting a sick friend of mine. He hasn't been able to call because he lost his charger and he told me to tell you not to worry and that he'll get a new one here in Dallas. We'll be heading your way in four or five days. Tell Mark I've got the cards in the trunk of my car and we'll have a good time looking at them when we get back. Raymond

Will it work? Have I covered everything? Will the daughter, M, believe it? It sounds a little too pat to me. Should I delete the sentence about the cards? If I don't mention them, it'll look like the men happily left town without getting what they came for. But if the cards are supposedly with Raymond on the way to Dallas, Roxy can't have them in her possession.

< 146 >

I've tolerated the criminal behavior in the building, neither condoning nor objecting. But this goes beyond passivity. This is the most heinous thing I've ever done. I read the email through five times before hitting send.

< 147 >

Unappreciated and Replaced

At around six-thirty I stop by Roxy's booth. She's gone for the day. The price tag dangling from the spit valve of the newly mounted trumpet reads four-fifty. Perching my backside on the stool behind her counter, I give her a call and tell her about the email to Humboldt's daughter from Raymond.

'So now, as far as anybody knows,' I tell her, 'they've moved on and they had the baseball cards with them. So we've got to get them out of your house.'

'How about I hide them until this blows over?' She exhales loudly and I imagine the cloud of smoke drifting around her head and through her kitchen, floating to the ceiling and hanging there.

'They're incriminating.'

'They're mine and I get to decide what to do with them.' What a pain she is. I should just let it go. No one's ever going to go out to her place looking for old baseball cards.

'I said you didn't have them anymore. We need to make that a reality. Why are you being so difficult?'

'Because I don't like being judged, I don't like being bossed around, and you're doing both.'

'Bring the baseball cards in tomorrow and I'll take care of them.'

I end the call. I've got a few minutes before meeting

< 148 >

Lizzie and Joe out back, so I return to the office and look up the price of trumpets.

The trumpet most closely resembling the one in Roxy's booth is a Bach Prelude. New, it sells for three hundred and ninety dollars.

'Jessica!' Lizzie's voice carries from the back exit. 'Joe's here. Let's go!'

Several vendors are still in the building. I'll lock up when I get back. Grabbing my purse, I head toward the sound of her voice.

I step outside to see Joe leaning against his drab Impala, with Lizzie bouncing and dancing around him. With each hop-and-twirl she declares a pizza ingredient – *Cheese! Pepperoni! Olives! Mushrooms! Onions! Sausage!* She's acting like a six-year-old.

Joe's changed to jeans and a T-shirt. With his arms wrapped across his chest he's got his eyes closed as if he's gone to a quiet place in his head.

I didn't lecture or reprimand Lizzie in any way about her clingy behavior when we went to the ball game. And she's as annoying tonight as she was then. She swings on Joe's hand when we walk from the car to the restaurant. She sits so close to him at the table that she's practically in his lap. She strokes his arm as he tries to eat. She talks nonstop about her new bike, her new flute, her new necklace. When she runs out of things to share about her life here, she tells him about Dayton – her friends, her teachers, her mother, her activities. And through it all Joe sends me nasty looks like he expects me to intervene, which I refuse to do.

Later, when we get home, Joe asks Lizzie to go inside so he and I can have a private conversation. She's reluctant, but she complies. Joe and I sit on the landing at the top of the outside stairs. Evenings in Caprock can be pretty great. The

< 149 >

wind, which pushed hard all day, has calmed to a soothing breeze; and the fierce sun has turned into a mellow red ball sinking into the horizon, turning the whole world pink and allowing the temperature to drop a few degrees.

'You're not going to help that girl at all, are you?'

'Her behavior is normal,' I say.

'Her behavior is obnoxious.'

'And that's normal.'

'She needs discipline and guidance. She needs someone to talk to who cares about her. And I still think she'd benefit from counseling.'

'Would it surprise you to know I don't give a rat's ass what you think?'

'No.' His elbows are propped on his knees and his hands are clasped between. I view his features in profile as he faces the end of the alley. The stubborn set of his chin reveals his disapproval. I remember this about him, how he always thought he knew best about what other people should do and how they should go about it. He lacks the ability to imagine any perspective other than his own, and this makes him a fool.

'She's not mine and she won't be here forever.'

'Her mother just left her here? If Child Welfare knew about this, she'd be taken into foster care.'

'How would they ever find out?'

'Do you want her here?'

'She's my husband's child.'

'Which doesn't answer my question.'

I stand, say goodnight, and go inside, leaving him sitting there. What makes him think he's entitled to any opinion at all about my life and my decisions?

Lizzie's sprawled on the couch, book hovering above her face.

< 150 >

'Are you enjoying that book? Isn't it pretty much the same as the last one you read?'

'If life was so hard during cowboy and Indian times, and people were starving and fighting all the time, why was it all the men seem to care about is having sex?'

'Maybe the book isn't giving an accurate picture.'

'Duh. That's why it's called fiction.'

Her phone is on the floor beside the couch. I still haven't mentioned to her that I spoke to Nicole. It gives a ding, alerting her to a text message. Within seconds, she's absorbed in communicating with her friends in Dayton.

I go down the interior stairs, intending to make sure the building is secure and the alarm is set.

All the second floor vendors have gone. Same on the ground floor. There's a light on in the basement and I go down to shoo whoever's still here out the door. It's Ken.

'Ken,' I call as I'm going down the stairs, 'it's time for you to close it down. I'm ready to lock up.'

I approach, scan the area. A dim illumination emanates from Audrey's Booth of Urns. She's left the low lighting on, which she's been instructed not to do.

The S of Ken's Superman T-shirt hangs across his sunken chest. He was a drinker back in the day, and his face attests to it – broken veins around his big red nose, yellow patches on his cheeks signaling liver damage, eyes permanently bloodshot. He moved in with Barry a few years ago. I have no idea why.

'Just puttering around,' he tells me.

He's perched on the stool behind his counter. Beside his right hand is a stack of comic books. Beside his left hand is a stack of the see-through envelopes that provide a protective layer between his merchandise and the grubby fingers of his geeky teenage customers. He slips a comic book into

< 151 >

an envelope and, standing, slumps toward the bins, flips through some tabs, and files it.

'Hey, I set aside something for that girly of yours.'

He separates out a comic book and holds it out to me. It's the Christmas issue of *Archie*, 1967.

'That's valuable, Ken.' I don't take it.

'It was meant to be enjoyed, not sit in some dark basement for the rest of its life.'

The rest of its life. He's imbued an inanimate object with mortality. With the utterance of this small phrase, the motivation behind this entire enterprise is clarified. The reason these people gather these things, display them like they're precious, and place such high prices on them is because they identify so closely with them.

Out of date, replaced, worn, unclaimed, unappreciated, destined for the trash heap.

'It'll mean more to her if you give it to her yourself.'

He shrugs, laying the *Archie* to the side.

'Want a beer?' he asks.

'Sure.'

He bends down, reaches into his small refrigerator, and pulls out a Coors.

'You been to see Will?' I accept the bottle, twist the cap, and down a swig.

'Barry and I dropped by the hospital last night.'

'And?'

'Ornery as ever. Looks like crap. Going home in a few days.'

'How do you feel about him and Sherman buying Pard's guns?'

'I don't know about that. But what I do know is, when Will's time comes, I've got dibs on that picture.' He thinks saying it will make it so. Dream on, Ken.

< 152 >

'That's not the way things work, and you know it. You think it's really a Norman Rockwell?'

'Darn tootin. Worth a fortune.'

If Ken were to get his hands on Will's alleged Norman Rockwell, just like with Will, it'd end up hanging in the prized position on the back wall of his booth. Unauthenticated and gathering dust. I bet Ken isn't the only person in the building with his eye on that painting. When Will dies, the first thing I'm going to do is get hold of the Coke folks, who've been calling it back home for years.

'Turn the lights out and let's get out of here.'

I walk him to the front of the building, let him out, lock the door behind him, and turn on the alarm.

Then I go to my office and print off a notice.

Concessionaires –
When you leave for the evening please turn off
all lights in your area. Failure to do so will result in
a five-dollar fine.

I post it on the front bulletin board.

< 153 >

Signs of Lizzie

'Everybody forgets to turn out the lights sometimes. And these folks are old. They tend to forget more than most. You can't charge them for it.'

Marlina is the fifth person to stop by. She talks about the others like they're old and she's not. Seeing her in my doorway reminds me how she's got fifty thousand in cash in a box in my safe.

'Haven't I heard you mention grandkids in Kentucky?'

The personal question draws a suspicious squint.

'I mean, you have someone in your family to see to your inventory when you're no longer with us, right?'

Broad-hipped and slow, Marlina rocks from side to side when she walks. Though she has knee pain, she refuses to use a cane. She sways in and sinks into the chair on the other side of the desk, grunting in relief when her backside takes her weight.

'What's with you lately?' she asks. 'Why are you going around asking everybody about wills and such? Is it something to do with your husband? Did he leave a mess behind? Were there unresolved issues when he passed on?'

'This has nothing to do with me.' My tone is cold as I shut down that line of thought. 'It rankles that I had no idea what Pard wanted. Did he have something in mind that didn't get done because he didn't let anybody know?

< 154 >

Surely he didn't want everybody squabbling over who got what like scavengers.'

'I think he might've gotten a kick out of it.' She talks about Pard like he was a man who found pleasure in things, which he most profoundly was not.

'Did he want his typewriters distributed throughout the building? I know for a fact that he and Abe couldn't stand each other – yet Abe's got one of Pard's typewriters right there on his counter. I'm pretty sure I saw him sneer at it yesterday. Would Pard have wanted that?'

'What he wanted was to take it with him, but sadly that wasn't an option.'

'He spent a lifetime choosing things to care about and gathering them in. It looks like he would've wanted to have a say in what happened to them.'

'Or maybe he didn't want to think about it. I still don't see how whether someone makes a will or has a plan is your business.'

'It's my business because I'm the one left in charge. And because I believe, when someone dies, it's important that their wishes are carried out.'

'And we're back where we started. This is about you. It has nothing to do with a bunch of senior citizens and what they leave behind. It has to do with you and your loss. Did your husband not have a will? Were you left to make decisions that you didn't know how to make? What did you do with your precious babies' things?'

'This conversation's over.'

I slap my hand on the desk, a percussive end to her intrusion. Pushing my chair back, I rise and stalk out, leaving her sitting in my office. Rushing to the stairs, taking them two-at-a-time, I burst into the apartment, where I pull out a chair at the table. And then just sit there, breathing hard

< 155 >

and fuming. What makes these grumpy used-up people think they can just talk about anything that pops into their heads?

Signs of Lizzie are everywhere. Her projects are taking over my home. On the surface in front of me the colorful puzzle is expanding inward from the corners. Beyond the puzzle, on the other side of the table, her flute is a long silver tube, laid out and ready for practice. The opposite chair is pulled out and turned toward the music stand, which holds the beginner's book open to the double page with the fingering chart. Further back, in the corner of the big room, her bed is made, but the rest of her area isn't neat. A couple of the drawers of the chest are open; the pinks and blues and greens that spill over offer a disorganized display of color that draws the eye. The cowboy potboiler rests open on its pages on her pillow so that the picture of the muscled torso and the overflowing bosom faces the ceiling.

Don left me everything. The house, the cars, the accounts, the insurance.

All his daughter got was an unthinking and uncaring mother, a mother so horrible, so selfish, that she handed over her child to someone who wanted nothing to do with her. I suppose, at some point, I should think about Lizzie and the money. I can't decide anything now; I'm not ready. But I do possess the nagging knowledge that she hasn't been treated fairly, an insistent truth that I won't be able to ignore for much longer.

Unlike Nicole, I was a perfect mother. I was dedicated, focused, educated, wise, sensitive, generous, patient. I had it in me to be a life-long encourager, a protector, an advisor. I was going to raise my girls to face the world on their terms, to be strong and independent, to be resilient when confronted by failure, to rely on their sharp brains and their

< 156 >

giving hearts. My girls were going to be respectful, charming, talented, kind, and brilliant.

They were mine to form, my little ones who were going to grow up and change lives.

And then they were gone.

Lizzie bursts in.

'She called!' Smiling like she'll never stop, she waves the phone and skips around, leaving a warm current of child sweat in her wake.

'Good. What did she say?'

'She's having a good time and she's learning a lot. She sounded real excited and happy. And she talked about how pretty Italy is and how she's made so many new friends.'

Sounds like Nicole had lots to share about what's going on in her life. The comparison is inevitable. Lizzie sounded the same way last night when she was going on and on to Joe about every little thing. The daughter is all about herself, just like the mother. On the other hand, Lizzie's twelve and Nicole's the adult; and I bet Nicole showed no interest in how her daughter's getting along.

'Did she say when she's coming back?'

'No, but we already know that. The end of July.' She gives me a funny look, like why would I be asking about something we already know?

It was at my instigation that Don and I made wills. When a couple has children, making a will is the responsible step. So I made the appointment and we went to a lawyer's office where we signed standard documents in which we named each other beneficiaries, with trusts set up for the girls. As far as Don was concerned, it was a waste of a Saturday afternoon. He thought death was something that only happened to old people who'd allowed themselves to wear out. And when we sat in that office listening as the

< 157 >

lawyer explained the various points, Don never once mentioned his daughter from his first marriage. Lizzie was far, far from his mind, an entity who really had nothing to do with him or us at all.

My phone rings and I dig it out of my pocket. It's Joe.

'We just got a call,' he tells me. 'Verney and Humboldt have moved on. They're in Dallas. So I don't have to bother that old lady anymore.'

'Good.'

'Verney sent an email to Humboldt's daughter. He said they got the baseball cards from his ex-wife – but ...'

'But what?'

'I'm still wondering – why would he leave his stuff in that hotel room?'

'He didn't officially check out, did he? Maybe he planned to stay there on his way back to Las Vegas.'

'He's not a rich man. People don't pay for hotel rooms they're not using.'

'That's true. Though it seems to me, people do things that don't make sense all the time.'

'Also, they wouldn't drive separate cars to Dallas, especially if they were coming back through here, so where's the extra car?'

'Are you asking me?' I forgot about Humboldt's car. I should have worked some plausible explanation into the email.

'It's hard to believe she handed the cards over to him and had no memory of it.'

'You saw what she was like. A lot of these folks can't remember what they said five minutes ago, much less what happened yesterday.'

'I don't know if I want to live so long that my brain turns to mush.'

< 158 >

'It's not like anybody has a choice. Thanks for letting me know. I'm glad not to have to put Roxy through that again.'

Yes, frail old Roxy, harmless, needy, brain all turned to mush. She'd better get those cards to me.

< 159 >

Death Trap

The ragged mountain of tornado debris still looms across the street. Splintered planks with nails poking out, fractured walls leaning precariously against one another, electric wires exposed and ripped and frayed – it's a hazard. The families that once lived there have been absorbed by the town, moved into other apartments, perhaps, or taken in by relatives. Ever since it happened people have been crawling around the lower edges of the heap, sorting through the more accessible wreckage, shifting broken doors and dented water tanks and metal sheeting, looking for anything salvageable. I recognize a few of the faces that once came and went regularly, but they don't come over to say hello or even to thank me for sheltering them that night. They're construction workers and cleaners and cafeteria servers. They didn't have insurance on their trucks and cars or beds and clothes. They've lost all the possessions that evidenced years of labor; gone is their material justification for dwelling in a foreign land that's so often hostile. I'm sympathetic, but they're idiots to be picking through the shards and rusty edges. It's just a matter of time until someone gets hurt.

'It looks like you managed to make Dee's daughter so mad that she's not talking to any of us,' Kathryn says as I approach her booth.

< 160 >

We both look toward Dee's booth where Tina is silently, rigidly, boxing up doilies and tablecloths and other lacy lengths of fabric. They've parked their home on wheels right across the front six parking places. Tina's husband fetches the packed cartons and disappears with them through the side door of the RV. A round-faced man, he looks uncomfortable wearing the frown his wife's forced on him. I wonder what they're going to do with the things Dee placed such value on.

'It's hardly my fault if her mother can't take care of herself anymore.'

'Blaming the messenger, that's what she's doing.'

Estelle thumps up the stairs and, seeing that we're having a gab, heads our way.

'They've already stuck her in a home.' Estelle's pitched her voice low so Tina won't hear, but the resentment comes through. 'They didn't even consider another option.'

'Wouldn't want them to miss one of their little cross-country jaunts.' Kathryn can be snide. 'I hear they've joined a caravanning club.'

They act upset about one thing when they're really upset about another. It's not Tina's putting Dee into a nursing home that's got them riled. It's the blatant and crude removal of Dee's stuff from the place it's been for the last thirty-or-so years. Each one of them thinks, for reasons I will never comprehend, that they have more right to Dee's stock than Dee's daughter.

We peer out the door, watching as the husband (don't know his name, never met him) climbs down the steps of the RV and returns to the building for another load. The view is mostly blocked by the huge vehicle, but movement at the far end of the window snags my peripheral vision.

Lizzie's on the other side of the street, tiptoeing her way

< 161 >

to the top of the rubble. Arms extended, back arched, she balances on a plank like a gymnast on the beam.

'Oh my God!' I go running – out the front door, across the parking lot, looking quickly both ways before leaping across the street, shrieking her name the whole way.

Eyes focused on her feet, she's working her way upward. Perils surround her. A jagged edge of a broken window pokes up on her right, menacing and streaked with filth. A rusty blade of corrugated steel lies across the plank, threatening her ankle. And what the hell? She's wearing flip-flops, no protection at all!

The board beneath her feet shifts and, abandoning the gymnast posture, she crouches, lowering her center of gravity.

'Lizzie!'

She turns, scowling down. 'What?'

'What you're doing is dangerous.' In an instant I've gone from hysterical to overly calm. 'I want you to turn around slowly and work your way back down.'

'I've seen loads of people over here.' She seems to think this is valid justification.

'And they're fools. Come on.'

'But there're all kinds of things in here, just waiting for someone to save them.'

'Lizzie, I mean it. Get back here.'

With a begrudging sigh, she carefully changes direction. She takes no more than two steps toward me when the board she's walking on tilts. She flails for a few seconds before regaining her footing.

'You okay?'

The board cracks and she sinks several inches. Her eyes get big. She reaches out, grasping the nearest support, which is a splintered two-by-four. She takes a sliding half

< 162 >

step. And another. And then the plank breaks the rest of the way and she crashes down into the mound of debris. The only thing that keeps her from plunging into the depths is her hold on the two-by-four. Her midsection is snagged on a rough edge of drywall.

'Help!' she yells.

I can't help her.

Arms straining as she hangs on to the fractured board, she drags her weight through the jagged maw.

'Are you alright?'

'I lost my shoes.'

She works her way to a hunkered position on the fragment of drywall and finds her balance. Barefoot now, she carefully continues picking her way down, emitting a tearful 'Ow!' with every foot placement. Surfaces are hot in the Panhandle in the summer and the bottoms of her feet are burning.

'Be careful of poking-up nails.'

'Duh.'

Blood is running down her lower leg. A big gash slashes across the side of her calf. I can't tell how deep it is.

She still has quite a way to go when she comes to a stable slab of concrete. She stops and turns her feet so they rest on their outer sides, giving temporary relief to the blistered bottoms. Bending over, spreading her palms on her knees, she hangs her head and starts crying. Then she takes her weight off her palms, looks at them, and cries even louder. I can't go get her. She's still quite high and there's a lot of wreckage between her and me.

'Lizzie, save the hysterics for later. Straighten up and get out of there.'

'I'm hurt.'

'Yes, you are, which is why you need to come on.'

< 163 >

I've got a better view of the cut on her leg. It's deep and long. Definitely stitches.

Straightening, she lifts her shirt, showing me. The tender skin of her abdomen is scraped raw where the rough edge of the wall caught her.

'Ouch,' I say. 'That's going to hurt for a while.'

After a few more sniffs she continues.

Kathryn and Estelle arrive.

'What was she thinking?' Kathryn huffs like she's just run a marathon.

Lizzie's almost down now; she's clear of danger.

'She wasn't. You two stay with her. I'm going to get the car.'

I run back to the building, through to my office where I grab my purse. Then I fly up the stairs to the apartment and rifle through the drawers in the kitchen, looking for the paper that gives me the right to get medical treatment for Lizzie. I just tossed it in somewhere. I never thought I'd have to use it. After finding it in the lowest drawer, I grab a clean towel, then cross to the safe and take out several hundred dollars. I race down the outside stairs and to the car. Driving around to the front of the building, I screech to a stop by Lizzie, who is once again on firm ground, standing on the outsides of her feet, and howling miserably in the double embrace of Kathryn and Estelle. I forgot to get her another pair of shoes.

As the two women help Lizzie into the passenger seat, I fold the towel and hand it to her.

'Press this to the cut on your leg.'

She complies. The front of her T-shirt is soaked red. She cries all the way to the emergency room.

Thirteen stitches. A tetanus shot. Dressing for the massive scrape that's taken several layers of skin off her

< 164 >

entire midsection. Cool packs for the first degree burns on her feet. Tweezer work and Neosporin for the splinters in her palms. And a single Tylenol with codeine.

Time: four hours.

Cost: three hundred and sixty-two dollars.

When we get home I point to Lizzie's bed and tell her to rest a while. I have no sympathy and no patience with her drama. She overplays the limp. She hunches protectively over her skinned stomach. She cuddles her arm where she got the shot. She moans over her tender palms. She whines. She groans. She insists I call Joe.

'He'll want to know I'm hurt,' she says. 'He'll want to come see me and give me a present.'

'Sure, I'll call him.' Not going to happen.

I dig a green shirt out of a drawer and toss it to her. She removes the bloody one and tosses it at me. It falls to the floor at my feet. I leave it there. She pulls the fresh one on over her head. Then she carefully relaxes into the mattress.

'You need anything?' I ask.

She closes her eyes, muttering something I don't understand.

'What?' I ask.

'I lost my phone when I fell through.'

'What were you thinking? What inside your brain told you it was okay to go climbing around over there?'

'I saw other people doing it.'

'They didn't go that high.'

'I figured the lower part was already picked clean.'

I leave her.

< 165 >

It's Done

Lizzie's risky adventure took up most of the day. It's five o'clock before I learn that Roxy never made it in, which means that she's still holding on to those stupid baseball cards. I can't believe something so foolish and insignificant is being so obstinately withheld. She's holed up out there in her little house, standing guard over them with a rapacious gleam in her eye and a club clutched in her arthritic fingers. Or she's hidden them in some odd place, gleefully and maliciously anticipating the pleasure of watching me search for them.

I see to some paperwork, then zip through the pick-up line at the Chinese take-out, ordering cashew chicken for Lizzie who, when I arrive home, is fretting over her lost phone. I paid the medical bill. Am I expected to replace her phone, too?

'How will Mom get hold of me? How will my friends let me know what's going on?'

'I have to go out for a while.'

'How will I get hold of you in case of an emergency when I don't have a phone?' Her squeaky voice indicates exhaustion, panic, and impending tears. She's making me crazy.

I settle her on the couch in front of the television, make sure her sexy cowboy book is nearby, and place her flute and

< 166 >

music stand within arm's reach. Her face is a bit flushed, but other than that she seems fine.

'Have you called the flute teacher yet?'

If she's not making demands about one thing she's making demands about another.

'I'll do it first thing tomorrow. You okay for a few hours?'

'My hands and feet hurt most. Then my stomach. The stitches in my leg hardly hurt at all, which doesn't make sense because that's my most serious worst thing.'

She turns her attention to the TV. Trying to sneak without being sneaky, I slide Arthur Humboldt's duffle bag from the safe and set it softly on the bed. Glancing across the room to make sure Lizzie's not looking my way, I remove the Beretta from the safe and add it to the duffle. I zip the bag closed and, hooking it over my shoulder, lock the safe and head toward the interior stairs.

'I could be back late,' I tell her as I slip out. As soon as I'm on the other side of the door I feel lighter. What an onerous, time-consuming, draining responsibility she is. Clambering around atop a twenty-foot-high mound of jagged metal and splintered boards – I never saw it coming. If there was one thing I thought I could count on with her, it was that she had a strong sense of self-preservation. What if she had died over there? What if she had hurt herself so badly that she lost a leg or an eye?

I descend through the building all the way to the basement, checking to make sure everyone's gone for the day. Returning to the ground floor, I stop at the office to add Raymond's iPad to the duffle bag. I liked the iPad. I might have to get one of those for myself. I exit through the rear door.

I've just tossed the bag in the back seat of my car when Joe's Impala turns the corner and rolls up the alley. He

< 167 >

doesn't turn into a parking place, but instead pulls up across the back of my car and lowers his window.

'Hey,' he says. 'Where are you on your way to?'

'Going to check on one of the vendors who didn't come in today.' Hoping he'll get the message that I want to be on my way, I open the driver's door. I feel like the incriminating bag is screaming at him from my back seat.

'Where's your shadow?'

'Upstairs watching TV.'

'I heard she had a bad day.'

'Yeah.'

'People her age don't have a lot of sense. She gonna be alright?'

'She'll live.'

'Is the well-being of these old folks a responsibility you've taken on? Do you always check on them when they don't show up?'

'If I don't, who will?'

'I'm thinking about the state of that old lady – well, I'd rather be dead.'

'Maybe you'll be lucky enough to die young.'

'One can always hope. See you later.' He raises his window as he drives away.

On the highway there's more traffic than usual; but when I take the turn to Roxy's, I lose the other cars. I've made this drive more often than I'd like lately, and each of those times it was during full darkness when the area presented a mysterious nocturnal charm. This time of day the glaring sun rides a quarter-inch above the western horizon, making long shadows out of stubby mesquite and fooling the eye into believing there are contours to the flat land. I suppose there's charm to be found in that as well, but I'm not in the mood.

< 168 >

Roxy's Camry is parked in front of her house, and I park next to it. The front door's closed. I climb the steps, tromp across the porch, and ring the bell. It takes her three minutes to answer. She cracks the screen door, opening it just a few inches so that half her face is blocked by the jamb. The single visible eye is accusatory. She doesn't invite me in.

'I came for the baseball cards,' I tell her, though of course she knows exactly why I'm here.

'I already got rid of them.'

'How?' I know her better than that.

'I burned them.'

'Where? Show me the ashes.'

'You don't believe me?'

'Not even a little bit. Roxy, they're just bits of printed paper. Even if they were worth something, you can't sell them because you're not supposed to have them. Please, just hand them over. Let me take care of this.'

I shove at the door, making her choose between retreating and being forced. She chooses resistance. I push hard and she pushes back. Hands splayed on the door, feet planted, we battle it out, but it's not much of a battle; she's a foot shorter than I am, and weak. Inevitably the door opens further and further until I'm fully inside; at which point, I let it go, the door slams, and Roxy falls on her face.

'Are you alright?' I ask without sympathy.

Prone on the floor, she emits a groan and turns over. Maybe her ribs are bruised, but her angry face as she glares up at me tells me that she'll live. She's wearing a house-dress, one of those oversized old ladies' garments I've seen on the racks that's a fusion of daytime clothes and night-time clothes. Swirling purple and green, it clashes with her pink hair.

< 169 >

The house smells like an ashtray.

I move to her head, stand over her, cup my fingers into her armpits from behind, and lift her to her feet.

'If I give them to you, what're you going to do with them?'

She places more value on those old cards than she did on two human lives. If I believed in such things, I'd say she's too close to the end of her life not to be agonizing over the assured prospect of hell.

'Toss them in the quarry, just like we did with Humboldt.'

She gasps as if I've stabbed her. Confused and desperate, she casts her eyes around the living room, looking for a plan. She inches along the wall, keeping space between us as though she thinks I'm going to attack her. The room is a small square, with one doorway leading to a hallway and another opening to the kitchen. On the opposite wall is a fireplace with a mantle of crumbling brick. If she had indeed burned the cards, that'd be where. I sniff; no, there's been no recent fire. Two chairs face away from the fireplace, toward the television, which sits on a rickety table. She slides behind one of the chairs.

'Alicia would never have treated me this way,' she says. 'She never disrespected any of us the way you're disrespecting me right now.'

My mother wasn't the saint Roxy's making her out to be. Mom could be stubborn and unforgiving and she often became furious over the most trivial things. But Roxy's right about one thing – my mother was compassionate and generous when it came to the vendors. Of course I've only recently learned how she could afford to be: she came into a fortune each time one of them died. In return she gave them rides, bought them meals, and listened for hours to their complaints about their aches and ailments and the

< 170 >

way their children and grandchildren never called or came to visit. And she gave them extensions on their rent for the silliest reasons. One thing I'm pretty sure she never did was help one of them get away with murder.

'Okay, how about this?' I ask, placating. 'I'll hold on to them for you. I'll keep them in the safe. You can have access to them any time you want, but they'll be out of your house.' It's a lie. Once I get them out of here, I'm destroying them.

By the fireplace now, she reaches down, grabs the poker, and yells 'Ah-ha!' as she brandishes it at me. With her wild pink hair and her billowing dress, she looks preposterous.

'You're kidding me.'

I disregard the weapon and take a step toward her.

She advances between the chairs and swings it wildly. I leap back, with the lethal point missing my nose by a couple of inches. Seizing a throw pillow from the chair on the left I fling it at her head, using the distraction to reach in and yank the poker from her knobby fingers. As I toss it aside, she comes at me with hands so puny and twisted that she's unable to make a proper fist. I straight-arm her, flattening my hand against her chest, holding her there as she flails and curses. I'm appalled, and furious, too, that she's forcing me to participate in the classic comedy sketch between the giant and the little guy.

Allowing her a step forward, I push her into one of the chairs, turn, and sit on her. Her limbs thrash for half a minute, then she goes still.

'Are you done?' I ask. 'Because I can sit here for the rest of the night.'

'I can't breathe.'

'Yeah, I imagine you can't. Where are they?' Silence. I wiggle and press my backside harder into her middle, restricting her ability to draw air, and ask again, 'Where?'

< 171 >

'You're crushing me.'

'You think I care?'

'The back bedroom.' A rough whisper.

I stand up and, without looking at her, go to the room at the end of the hall. I turn on the light, slumping when I see what I'm up against. Every surface is taken up with some sort of worn-out useless item. Dented lampshades, wrecked furniture, flattened pillows, broken appliances. A professional hair dryer, the kind that's attached to a cushioned chair, takes up a corner and is stacked high with faded towels. Two bed frames lean against one wall, while a twin mattress set leans against the other. Stuff, stuff, stuff everywhere. I pick my way to the center of the room, coming to a halt between a fractured cabinet and a sprawled bundle of yellowed window shades. Helpless, not knowing where to start, I scan the area.

Roxy scowls from the doorway. I don't know where in this mess the cards are. I give her a questioning look.

'You think I'm going to help?' Incensed and humiliated, she's going to hate me forever. 'You want 'em so bad, find 'em yourself.'

She turns and shuffles away, her slight limp an indication that the scuffle she instigated has taken its toll.

It takes me half an hour of looking under and behind all this worthless crap to find the cards. They're in a packing box in the back of the closet, buried under a couple of years' worth of magazines from the 1980s. I clear a space on the cracked surface of a nearby end table, open the box, and peer in. Men in baseball caps smile up at me as the odor of aged dust and mildew assaults my eyes and nose. I estimate five hundred cards. Ken would be appalled to see this. He sorts his collection according to position, teams, year, statistics. He carefully slips tiny transparent sleeves on

< 172 >

every card and inserts cross-reference information in the filed bins. These cards were simply dumped into the box. Not organized, not properly preserved, just dropped negligently. How could Roxy care so much about something that she obviously doesn't care about at all?

I replace the lid, take the box in my arms, and carefully work my way back through the disordered by-products of the old woman's entire adult life.

I march back through the house and out to the car. Roxy's made herself scarce, which is fine by me. I slide the box of cards into the back seat next to the duffle bag and drive away.

Once again, the quarry in the dark.

There are plenty of big rocks strewn around the border of this flat area where I've parked. I gather twenty fist-sized orbs of granite, zip them into the duffle, and swing it over the cliff. The splash is barely audible. Shining my flashlight down, I confirm that it's sinking before I pick up a couple dozen more rocks and drop them into the box with the cards. Foreseeing the need, I brought twine. I replace the lid, wrap the twine around the box several times in opposing directions, tie it off and, dropping it over the edge, listen to the distant *shosh*. I enjoy the thought of the water soaking into the cardboard. How long will it take for the cards to turn to mush? Two days? A week? Even with the rocks to add weight, the box bobs on the surface for several minutes before it begins to become waterlogged. It takes twenty minutes before it is heavy enough to sink.

On the way home I ponder how pointless this excursion was. Two good men dead. And I got distracted by baseball cards. It was the principle that grabbed me, a lame attempt to achieve balance. Roxy killed for the cards and so they had to go. It's done.

< 173 >

Old Men Being Foolish

Lizzie's moving slowly this morning, exaggerating her achy injuries with admirable skill.

Sitting in my chair behind the desk, she scrolls through the websites, researching phones and dropping hints. Sitting opposite, I'm doing the same thing on the laptop, only I'm checking out iPads instead of iPhones.

'I can keep my old number,' she says.

Kathryn enters. A couple of weeks ago she stopped wearing regular shoes on her feet and began wearing only soft house shoes; an enlightening fashion choice, but not my concern. Now every step she takes is accompanied by a *foosh* as the soles slide along.

'How's our injured girl today?' she asks.

'I hurt all over,' Lizzie says with a beautiful pout, a flawless blend of pain and sadness.

'I brought you a little cheer-up present.' Kathryn places a miniature cream pitcher on the desk. Only two inches tall, pink and delicate, it's the perfect item to fascinate a twelve-year-old girl. Lizzie strokes the smooth china appreciatively.

Estelle comes through the door. She, too, has an offering – a ball-and-cup set.

'Here,' she says. 'Something to keep you entertained while you're getting better.'

< 174 >

Lizzie accepts the toy and immediately swings the ball out and around, trying to catch it in the cup.

'I love both these things.' Polite and gracious. If there's one thing this child knows, it's how to accept gifts. 'Thank you.'

Will strides in with an attitude. He glares at the two women until they get the message and hurry out, bumping into each other in the doorway and sending anxious glances at me before they turn the corner. Will wasn't the most robust specimen before he got pneumonia and he looks worse now. The plum-colored bruise that covered half his face last time I saw him has yellowed around the edges and he's lost several pounds. Yesterday's rumor that he was being released this morning was obviously true. I wonder if he came straight here from the hospital.

'You look awful.' I close the laptop, place it on the desk, and stand. Indicating that he should take the chair, I turn and prop my backside on the desk so that I'm facing him. 'How're you feeling? Shouldn't you be at home in bed?'

'You stole the carpet from my booth. You got no right.'

'Let's not have this argument.'

He tosses a handful of bills next to me on the laptop. The guns again. Seeing the amount, Lizzie's eyes go big. Think how many phones that'd buy.

'Okay, I see you've got it. I see you're serious. Now pick this money up off my desk,' I say, knowing that if I touch it I'll be accepting his terms.

Reluctantly, and with difficulty because his fingers are stiff and clumsy, he reaches out and gathers the bills. Clutching them in his gnarled fist, settling back again, he gives me a squint that's meant to be intimidating, but comes off as petulant.

'You have yet to assure me that you'll get them off my property.'

< 175 >

'Where is it you think we should put them?'

I'm not supposed to know about Will's storage units so I can't mention them, but they're sure on my mind. Why can't they keep them there? Has he forgotten about them? No, of course not. Secretive and suspicious, he doesn't want Sherman to learn about his private treasures. This is the mind-set that's at work here. These old guys are entering into some kind of shady weapons-based partnership; and at the same time, they're stuck in the days when they were swaggering cocks competing for money and women.

'I don't care where you store them. I just want them out of here.'

'What we keep in our booths is up to us. Your mother never poked her nose in.'

This has gone on long enough. If their plan was to wear me down, they've succeeded. There was a time when I had the energy to be tenacious, but any resolve I once possessed has been replaced by the resigned knowledge that I have no control over anything.

'Okay.' I hold out a palm, signaling with my fingers for him to give me his damned money. 'But you're getting eleven, not twelve,' I override his protest. 'Take it up with Sherman. He knows why.'

I accept his money, straighten the bills into a fat stack and, after making a show of placing them in the safe, tell him I'll hand over their new property at the bottom of the back stairs in an hour. My phone rings as he struts out the door, proud, telling himself he's still got it. I extract the phone from my pocket and glance at the screen. It reads Unknown Caller, which I take to mean Nicole.

'Hi, Nicole.' At the mention of her mother's name, Lizzie hops up, squeals, and flashes her hand out like she's going to snatch my phone. I turn away from her, hunching over.

< 176 >

'Hi, yourself.' Nicole's cheerful tone makes me mad.

'Your daughter fell into a massive pile of rubble,' I tell her. 'She needed stitches in her leg and a tetanus shot and she scraped several layers of skin off her stomach.'

'Ouch, poor thing. But she's a strong girl. I'm sure she's alright.'

'You owe me three hundred and sixty-two dollars.'

'I'll write you a check first thing when I get back.' Sure she will.

'Why are you calling, Nicole?'

'Just to check in. A little something's come up.'

'Oh?'

'Just a little trip is all. I'm going to Rome for a few days. I thought I should let you know.'

'How responsible of you.'

'Oh, and I just have to tell you about this wonderful – '

When I hear the word 'wonderful' I end the call.

'That's it?' Lizzie asks, dismayed. 'Why didn't you let me talk to her?'

I don't know why I didn't hand the phone to Lizzie. Nicole's lack of concern over her daughter's injuries made me angry. Doesn't she love her little girl at all? What is their home life like in Dayton? Has Nicole ever, once, put her daughter's needs before her own?

'I'm sorry,' I say. 'I didn't think. I'll do better next time.'

With Lizzie tagging along, prattling about her phone needs, I go to the bank and exchange fifteen hundred in big bills for fifteen hundred in small ones.

'Why'd that guy give you all that?' she asks as we drive back from the bank.

'Because he's senile and it's just the way we do things.'

A while later, after I send Lizzie off to tell Sue that it'll be a couple of days before she can make any bike deliveries, I

< 177 >

go upstairs and load Pard's guns into a hard yellow suitcase that's so old it's held closed with clasps and it doesn't have wheels. I lug it down the back stairs and hand it over to Will and Sherman, who're waiting at the bottom. They each take a firm grasp on the short handle, squeezing their hands so close together that their fingers turn purple. They're determined to share every aspect of ownership. Walking away with a clumsy opposing stride, each step is a tug-of-war, with the suitcase rising and falling between them. It's like watching a really bad slapstick scene. And where do they go with their newly acquired booty? Right back into the building.

The two of them sharing possession will never work. They're both too petty and too paranoid. So they'll eventually realize they've got to work out a split. One of them will get six of the guns, and those will end up tucked into a bottom drawer, or placed in a crate and shoved into a corner. The other will get five guns, plus the suitcase and a little extra money because the suitcase isn't worth as much as a gun; and these guns will remain in the suitcase, which will also be dropped in an out-of-the-way corner or pushed under a counter. They'll promise each other that when one of them dies, the guns'll go to the remaining partner. But there'll be no documentation to that effect.

In calculating the distribution of the money, I divide the sum by the number of vendors, figuring in a double portion for myself because, well, I've simply decided that's the way it should be. Then I walk around the building, handing out thirty-two dollars to every vendor that's come in today. By the end of the day, thirty out of the forty-six have received their portion of the payment for Pard's guns.

It'll take a few days to distribute the portions to the remaining vendors, but after that it'll be over and done with.

< 178 >

On and On and On

'I think it was Abe who did it.'

'Did what?'

'Warn Sylvia that we moved the typewriters around.'

I thought it was a dead issue, but apparently people are still mulling. Usually the vendors don't involve me in their rumors and schemes, but for some reason Marlina's decided to stop in for a gossip. This is the second morning this week that she's come in, and this time she brought me a coffee from Koffee Klatch, an uncharacteristically generous act that makes me wonder why she's really here.

'What makes you think it was him?'

'They've just seemed cozy lately.' Cozy. Not a word I'd apply to bony Abe, with his liver spots and few strands of white hair – or to Sylvia, whose spine's so crooked she'd break in two if she tried to look him in the eye.

'Why are you here, Marlina? Why did you bring me coffee?'

'That right there's your problem. You're too suspicious. You need to lighten up, be more friendly.'

'I'll take it under advisement.'

'See?' She smacks her lips in a condescending way. 'Your tone right then was snide. Also, you need to take us seriously when we bring you a problem or a complaint. We pay rent, we deserve some consideration.'

< 179 >

'You've got something specific on your mind. Let's have it.'

'It's about the way you divided the money. Audrey's new. She didn't even know Pard. She didn't deserve a share.'

'Oh, for the love of God.' Some things just go on and on and on.

'I mean it. You should have consulted with someone before you arbitrarily decided how to divide up that money.'

'How about, next time I'll come find you and you can tell me what to do and how to do it – how does that sound?'

'I can't tell if you're being sarcastic or sincere.'

'Definitely sincere.' Not.

'Okay then.' Her achy knees crack as she hauls her heavy backside from the chair. At the door she turns and says, 'And another thing. It's not right that just because Sue bought that child a bicycle, she gets to monopolize all her time. I got chores I wanted her to do. She could be making money off any number of us, but Sue won't let go of her. Right now the poor child's digging out the dust from every fold in those old bellows of Pard's – bellows, I might add, that Sue had no right to, but just went in and took for herself.'

She continues out the door. They all claimed something from Pard's booth. Marlina ended up with a handmade basket that she's filled with colorful mismatched saucers from the thirties – it makes a cute display. Yet she resents Sue for doing the same thing.

A glance at my watch reminds me that it's almost time for Lizzie's flute lesson. When I find her, she's doing exactly what Marlina described – hunching over a set of bellows and scraping deeply imbedded grunge from its folds with the pointed tip of a nail file. Sue's nowhere in sight.

'Where's Sue? Did she leave you manning her booth? Because it's almost time for your flute lesson.'

< 180 >

'She had to make a delivery. And because that's supposed to be my job, she left me here doing this. I have to clean this thing and watch her booth and she's not even paying me for it. And it's not like she's got any customers.'

'She did give you a bicycle.'

'But I can't help that I'm hurt. And she pays me for the deliveries, so why shouldn't she pay me for doing this?'

Heading toward the back, Carly changes direction when she sees me at Sue's.

'You seen Roxy?' she asks. 'Looks like she had a run-in with the business end of a baseball bat.'

'What?'

'Ran into a door, she says, but I'm not buying it.'

I ask Carly if she'll keep an eye on Sue's booth. I tell Lizzie to get herself upstairs for her lesson, hollering after her to wash her hands and brush her teeth first. Then I go to check on Roxy, who, it turns out, does indeed look like somebody went after her with a bat. Beat-up looks bad on anybody, but it looks horrific when the victim is a tiny ancient woman. The whole right side of her face is swollen and covered in different shades of purple, a gruesome contrast to her pink hair. There's a gash on her brow and her eye is swollen shut. The bright bruise travels down her neck and disappears beneath the collar of her blouse. And though she's wearing long sleeves, bright bruises are visible beneath the cuffs, giving the impression of an under-the-skin downward flow of blood. Finger marks are clearly outlined in the thin layer of flesh at her wrists.

'Roxy Lynn, what the hell? Who did this to you?'

'That Humboldt must've gone all over town talking to every friend Raymond ever had.' The swollen eye renders a Popeye effect. 'And one of those people was my first husband's brother, Rook.'

< 181 >

'The brother of the husband you killed was friends with your next husband?'

'Yeah, and not only did he tell Rook that he was looking for Raymond – he told him about me having some valuable baseball cards. So last night who should come knocking, but Rook, who hates me and thinks I owe him, and he was demanding I give him those cards.'

'What did you tell him? Did you tell him they were in my safe?' As far as she knows, that's where they are – in a safe that's downstairs from where I sleep, from where Lizzie sleeps.

'I told him I gave them to a friend for safekeeping. And then he said for me to fetch them and he'd be back for them tonight.' Her sneaky expression morphs into one of bull-headed determination as she adds, 'But if he thinks I'm giving him those cards, he better think again. So you just keep them right where they are.'

'This is never going to end, is it?'

'That old boy needs to learn a lesson. People need to leave me and my stuff alone.'

'Let me call Joe. You need to file charges against this guy.'

'I never in my life turned to a cop for help and I'm not going to now. I need the Beretta again.' She doesn't know that her gun-of-choice is long gone.

'I'm not in charge of the firearms anymore. You're going to do what you're going to do, but I'm out of it.'

'You sold to Will and Sherman? Where's my share?'

'I'll get it to you. I mean it, Roxy. Whatever happens, I don't want to know.'

'Yeah, I heard. You're out of it.' She's bitter.

'Take care of yourself.' I give a farewell tap on her counter before turning away.

I walk back through the building. Dee's empty booth

< 182 >

makes me sad. It's one of the front units, a prime location. It won't be long before the vendors start squabbling over who should get it.

Climbing the stairs, I cross to the opposite side of the building, walk up the aisle to Will's booth, and scan his area. Easy to spot because it's the only thing in the booth that's not red and white and covered in dust, the yellow suitcase is tucked into the right rear corner between the shelves of Coke bottles and the back partition. I know what to expect. I enter his area, lift the suitcase, and measure its heft. It weighs the same as it did yesterday, which means the two men haven't reached the point of dividing them up. Will is nowhere in sight.

I put the suitcase back. I wonder how much he and Sherman are going to charge Roxy to rent a gun for the night. Or hey, maybe they'll rent it to her for a full week, like I did.

< 183 >

Old Thugs

'If you mention that phone one more time before this day's over, you can just forget about ever getting another one. I'm sick of hearing about it.'

What a stupid thing to say. I've implied that if she goes the evening without bringing up her lost phone, I'll buy her a new one. We've just been to the grocery store. Our dinner tonight will be fried chicken and a pasta salad, both of which we bought at the deli counter. The warm greasy aroma of the chicken drifts through the car.

'Does that mean if I quit talking about it, we can get me a new one tomorrow?'

Yep, saw that one coming.

'How'd the lesson go?'

'I like my new teacher. She says I have natural ability.'

She probably does. I've always assumed she was an average kid, but I'm coming to realize she's pretty sharp, most likely upper ten percentile on the smart chart.

'Will you get started on your required reading if I read it along with you?'

'Last year there were four books on the summer list and we only ever talked about one of them in school, and the teacher made us read it again as a group. We spent a month rereading something we'd already read.'

'I don't know how to respond to that.'

< 184 >

'And we never even discussed the other ones. It was a waste.'

'But still, don't you think it's better to be prepared than not? This year's teacher might expect you to have done what you were supposed to do. She might give a test on the material the very first day. Honestly, you never know.'

'Why didn't you let me talk to Mom yesterday when she called?'

'I said I was sorry. Let's just move on.'

I terminated the call because I was disgusted with Nicole. I didn't think about Lizzie at all.

'But it makes me sad to think that my phone is buried over there and it's probably ringing and ringing because you told Mom I was hurt and she's calling to check on me. But you didn't tell her I lost my phone and she'll be worried when I don't answer.'

She brought it up again, so technically I'm off the hook. But she's near tears.

'Here.' I take my phone from the console and hand it to her. 'When she can't get hold of you she'll call me. It's not like that many people call me. And if they do, it's usually somebody I don't want to talk to in the first place.'

'Really?'

'Go for it. Text to your little heart's content.'

What have I let myself in for? I'm going to be receiving messages from Dayton's twelve-year-olds for the next year.

It doesn't take long before she's focused on nothing but the phone. It's in her hand or next to her until bedtime, and then she places it on the nightstand, overly careful in her handling, as though it's fragile, precious, irreplaceable.

Someone pounds on the door around midnight, yanking me from sleep, causing my heart to leap and race. I turn on the light. Lizzie, too, has been startled.

< 185 >

'What! What is it?' She snaps to a sitting position. Her hair is wild and her brown eyes are wide and glazed from being pulled out of deep slumber.

'Stay where you are.' I motion her back down. 'I'll take care of it.'

Pulling my gray sweater over the sleeves of my pajama top, slipping my feet into flip-flops, I rush across the room. Lacking a peephole, I holler through the door.

'Who is it?'

'Roxy.'

'Go away, Roxy Lynn. Whatever it is can wait until morning.'

'Open the door.'

There's more pounding and, irritated, I sling it open.

Roxy looks even worse than she did earlier. She's taken another blow to the other side of her face and her blouse is ripped at the shoulder. Bleary-eyed, like she's having trouble focusing, she sways between two scruffy men.

'This here's Rook and Cameron.' She gestures weakly.

Cameron's kind of old – mid-sixties; and Rook's really old – probably eighty-five. Both have the same protruding lower lip, bulbous nose, and similar slope to their shoulders. Father and son. Cameron clutches a gun, which he points at me, then at Roxy, then back at me, then back to Roxy. Terrifying and surreal. Two puny old men – how dangerous can they be, really?

'Give us the cards. We know you've got them.' Rook's voice is a growl and his breath is rotten. He looks frail, but his grip on Roxy's arm is strong.

'You brought these thugs to my home?' I glare at Roxy.

'I only expected Rook, but this other one came up behind me.' Her words are slightly slurred. She seems to be struggling to stay alert.

< 186 >

'They aren't here,' I tell the men. 'They're downstairs.'

I can't think straight. I suppose I said this because it's what I told Roxy. The main thing is, I've got to get these creeps away from here, away from Lizzie. As there are no cards, maybe I can send them away with money. I slide outside, crowding on to the landing, pulling the door closed behind me as I struggle to come up with a plan.

In an attempt to show how badass he is, Rook jerks Roxy back and forth a little bit. She gasps and clutches her wrist to her breast.

'Stop! You're hurting her! They're in the safe in my office.'

With Rook maintaining his hold on Roxy's arm, and the one with the gun taking up the rear, we troop down the narrow steps. The skimpy sandals slap my feet with every step. At one point Roxy nearly stumbles and the old guy, none too gently, keeps her on her feet. We're at the back door when I remember I don't have the key card.

'The key's upstairs,' I say, turning back. 'I'll go get it.'

Cameron follows me up, stomping loudly and complaining the whole way. We reach the third story stoop. All it'd take would be a little shove, just a pivot-and-push, and this lowlife'd go flying backwards down the metal staircase. I picture it in my head – my full force behind an elbow to his flabby midsection, a vicious tumble down sharp-edged surfaces, and a broken neck at the bottom. But I hesitate, scared to act, and he reaches around me, turns the knob, and shoves me inside. He follows, but stays in the doorway.

Lizzie's not in her bed. She's probably under it. Good girl.

I go straight to my purse, which hangs by its strap on a chair. I grab the card from the outer pocket and rush back to the door. We go back down the two flights to where Roxy's waiting with her captor.

< 187 >

I open the back door, move to the panel, and poke in the code. Then we're in.

I'm only allowed a second to test the atmosphere. I harbor desperate hope that someone's in the building. Sometimes Barry takes midnight deliveries. Sometimes Ken stays late. Sometimes old folks who can't sleep sneak in and move typewriters around. But I made the rules, and now I have to live with them. No one checked out a key today. No late-night shenanigans are going on. The building is empty.

'Move it,' comes from behind.

I lead them to the office and turn on the light.

The safe stands before us, impressive in that it takes up almost half the back wall. I'm going to have to tell them that the cards aren't here. I can offer them cash, though.

A picture of Marlina pops into my head; a heavy woman with arthritic knees. She gave me coffee and an unsolicited lecture just this morning. Fifty thousand of her dollars are in this safe. I imagine she loves that money more than she ever loved a human being.

These two goons may get out of here with thousands of dollars, but what kind of caretaker would I be if I just handed it over?

'Go on.' Cameron aims the muzzle toward the safe, then to me, then to the safe. He holds it sideways, like a TV drug dealer – but something's not right; the back-and-forth motion seems to be masking a significant tremor.

'I have to find the combination.'

I'm not going to make it easy for them, but the only thing I can think to do is stall. I move to the other side of the desk and settle into my chair. What will a bullet burning through my flesh feel like? I open the top drawer and rifle through paper clips and rubber bands. My hands are trembling almost as badly as Cameron's.

< 188 >

Closing this drawer, I open the bottom one, and flip through the files.

'Quit messing around and open it!' Up and down with the gun.

'Please understand. I want to do this for you. But I don't use it that often and I haven't memorized the combination. Be patient and I'll have it open in a jiffy.' Jiffy. Not a word I use in the ordinary course of a day.

He draws circles in the air with the muzzle. If he holds his hand still for a few seconds, the whole gun starts vibrating. This is not a healthy man. Sweat tickles my scalp, but I feel cold all over.

I lift out a file, open it, act as if I'm scanning, close it, and replace it in the drawer. Then I do it again.

Rook gives Roxy another shake.

'Please quit doing that. She's hurt.' Fear has added a wobble to my voice. 'Why don't you let her sit down?'

'No way does this murdering bitch sit.' He yanks her back and forth so that her head flops.

'Roxy, you alright?' I ask, concerned by the way she's swaying.

'Just get to it,' Rook says.

I pretend to come across a piece of paper with the code written on it. I stand, circle the desk, approach the safe, and twirl the lock face. The latch releases and I open the door.

'They're in one of these boxes, but I'm not sure which one.'

I lift Pard's box out, cross back to the desk, and make a show of digging out and inserting the key. Lifting the lid, I reveal the out-of-date receipts and warranties.

'Well, this obviously isn't it,' I say apologetically.

I'm dragging it out as much as I'm able. I return the box to the safe, replace Pard's box, reach for Will's, and –

< 189 >

Bang!

Something shatters above my head. I fall to the floor. Glass rains down.

'Idiot. What'd you do that for?'

'I didn't mean to. My damn hand shakes so.'

I look for pain. None comes. I'm fine.

'You've drawn attention.'

'Naw, this building's solid.'

'You! Get up and get this thing done.'

I uncurl, rise. My knees are weak. I hold the door of the safe for support. A faded print of an eighteenth-century garden party has been shot. Shards of the cover glass are all over me, the floor, the safe – but the framed picture still hangs, only now there's a hole right through one of the women's faces.

'Hurry. We haven't got all day.'

Breathing, pulling myself together, I take Will's box and return to my place behind the desk, going through the charade again.

Joe bursts into the room, weapon drawn, like a movie hero. He orders Cameron to put the weapon down.

I collapse, forehead to desk.

I hear what's going on, but from a distance. I'm frozen this way, eyes closed. I hear footsteps as more officers hustle in. Then – voices barking commands; the clink of cop gear; bitter old-man accusations against Roxy; the reeling off of the rights.

'You okay? You doing alright?' Joe asks, placing a hand on my shoulder.

I force myself to lift my head, open my eyes. Rook and Cameron are handcuffed, being led from the room. Without Rook to hold her up, Roxy has collapsed into the chair. She drops her head to her chest with a rough sigh.

< 190 >

'Lizzie called,' he tells me.

Wearing a white shirt and dark trousers, the poorly fitted jacket is gone, revealing the shoulder holster. Circling the desk as he slips his gun into the empty holster, he squats in front of Roxy, and places three fingers across the side of her throat to check her pulse. He peers at her face. Her eyes are closed. She remains unmoving.

'Hey, you alright? An ambulance is on its way.' He turns and asks, 'What's this ole gal's name again?'

'Roxy.'

'Roxy, you hear me? Open your eyes and look at me.'

She collapses forward, falling into his arms.

I pick up the desk phone and call my cell.

'Are you okay?' Anxiety causes Lizzie to squeak.

'We're fine. You did good.'

Ten o'clock tomorrow morning will find me at the mall buying this girl an iPhone, along with any case she wants, and if there's any other accessory she wants, I'll buy that, too.

< 191 >

Roxy's New Reality

I look up the seventh grade summer reading list for Dayton. Four titles; I'm familiar with each; and I'm pretty sure Lizzie will enjoy every one of them. These books are well written, relevant to the human condition, and appropriate for her age.

I look up the reading list for the Caprock seventh graders. Also four titles, two in common with the Dayton list.

I order the latest Kindle from Amazon, paying extra for it to arrive quickly, fully charged, and pre-loaded with the six books from the reading lists. I'll slap it into her hands the second she finishes her cowboy sex book.

Sue pokes her head in.

'That little klepto of yours stole one of my birds.' One of Sue's central displays is the complete collection of Lenox garden birds. She loves them, but I don't get the appeal.

'You had her working your booth yesterday without pay. She probably took it in lieu of wages due.'

'You're saying it's okay for her to steal?'

'No, but it's not okay to take advantage of a kid, either. She could've been earning from one of the other vendors. She needs the money.'

'I bought her that bicycle and now she's hurt and can't do the job I hired her to do.'

I'm sleep-deprived, Roxy's in the hospital, and Joe's going

< 192 >

to be here any second to grill me about that gun he netted last night. And she's making my bad mood worse.

'This is not a good time for this,' I tell her. 'I'll get your little bird back to you. But for right now, I think it'd be best if you just turn and walk away.'

That was bitchy. She straightens, emits an indignant sniff, does an about-face, and marches away.

I call the hospital to check on Roxy and am transferred to the station on her floor. When the nurse identifies herself as Patrice Boyd, I'm pleased to be in contact with a friend from high school. We share a few minutes of catch-up chit-chat, then she looks up Roxy's records.

'She regained consciousness early on,' she tells me, 'so that's good. But her speech is slurred, her vision's fuzzy, and she seems confused. In addition to the head trauma, she has a broken wrist.'

'Confused how?'

'Doesn't know where she is or how she got here. Doesn't know where she was born, what month it is, who the president is. That kind of thing.'

'Isn't that normal with a head injury?'

'Every case is different. Her age is a factor. She wasn't in great shape to start with.'

'What happens next?'

'We'll run tests. And who knows – she might snap out of it later in the day. But I'll tell you one thing – once someone's stuck on the senior conveyor belt, they hardly ever get off it.'

I thank her and end the call. The senior conveyor belt. That's one way to put it. My mother dealt with these elderlies for most of her adult life, and, by extension, so did I. Unless Roxy shows immediate improvement, social services will be called in to oversee her care. From the hospital she'll

< 193 >

go into a rehab/nursing facility where she'll be thoroughly assessed. Therapists will be called in to help her regain her strength and coordination. But in the rehab center improvement is a hope rather than an actuality. No one improves. No one gets to go home. From there the next step is always a nursing home. People she doesn't know will hand her pills, and she won't know what the pills are or why she's taking them. At meal-times she'll be led, or wheeled, to a communal area full of drooping people who wear bibs. And the confusion that only a few days ago was feigned will become her new reality. Poor Roxy.

A light tap on the doorjamb interrupts my thoughts. It's Audrey, the urn collector.

'Hey, Audrey. What can I do for you?'

'I don't know what your policy is for switching locations, but I think my business'll pick up if I move to that booth close to the front door, the one that just came empty.'

Dee's booth. I knew it wouldn't be long.

'But you just got your area set up. Construction was involved.' I motion her toward the chair on the other side of the desk.

'It won't take half a day to move the shelving up from the basement.' She enters and takes the seat.

'If I let you have that booth half the vendors in the building'll be knocking at my door, griping about it.'

'But I'm the first to ask, right?'

'This isn't necessarily a first-come situation. Some'll think it's a matter of seniority, that whoever's been here longest should have dibs. But if you ask me, it's all about the money.'

'What do you mean?' She looks wary, which lifts my spirits a little.

'It's going to the highest bidder.' A brilliant idea. This'll

< 194 >

get 'em riled. They need something new to complain about. When she's gone I print a notice.

Concessionaires –
   Because of the large number of requests for occupation of booth 1B, I'm opening a bid round. Bids are due before closing on Friday. Questions? See me.
Jessica

I post the notice, return to the office, and prepare to be overrun. But the next person to knock on my door isn't a vendor – it's Joe.

'How're you doing?' Joe enters and flops into the chair. He crosses an ankle over a knee and releases an exhausted sigh.

'I'm tired and cranky,' I tell him.

'Nothing new there. Rook and Cameron Arckle. What do you know about them?'

'Roxy killed Rook's brother. From what I saw, he hated her.'

'Yeah, I got that much.' He shifts, reminding me that I want him gone.

'Arthur Humboldt told me that Roxy was his only lead in finding Raymond,' I say. 'Maybe when he saw how out of it she was, he took his search elsewhere.' The one time they'd met she'd been perfectly lucid, but Joe doesn't know that.

'Rook and Raymond used to be friends, back before Raymond married Roxy.'

'So it makes sense that Humboldt would ask Rook if he knew Raymond's whereabouts.'

'But why would he tell Rook about the baseball cards?'

'People have conversations. Maybe they bonded. You've got Rook in custody, why don't you ask him?'

< 195 >

'Do you have the cards?'

'How could I have them? Didn't you tell me they were in Dallas?'

'Then why did the Arckles think you had them?'

'I guess that's what Roxy told them. She's been getting more and more confused lately. Also, I don't think he cared about any cards. I think it was about Rook wanting to take something off Roxy. When Humboldt put Roxy on Rook's radar, Rook got mad at her all over again. He's an old man who wanted to get even.'

'They said they took the gun off her.'

'Why are you here?'

'Where would that old woman have gotten a gun?' What kind of naiveté allows him to believe that guns are rare and difficult to obtain? As far as I can see, guns are everywhere.

'I have no idea.'

'You never heard anything about Pard Kemp's guns?'

'No.'

'There's no chance Roxy got it from Pard?'

'How the hell would I know?'

'And the baseball cards left town with Verney and Humboldt, right?'

'Is there reason to believe differently?'

'I've just come from the hospital and she's as muddled as ever.'

'Did you think getting beat on the head would give her sudden clarity?'

'How's Lizzie?'

'She's been stealing from the vendors and I bought her a new phone this morning.'

'You don't think that's sending a mixed message?'

'I really don't care.'

'Let me know if you hear anything about guns or baseball

< 196 >

cards. See you later.' He pulls himself to his feet, groaning like he's thirty years older than he is. With a wave, he saunters out.

My phone gives a ding. Lizzie had my phone for approximately fourteen hours and so far today I've had at least a dozen text messages from girls in Dayton. I'm looking at it, exasperated, when it rings. It's the hospital.

'Hello?'

'Hi, Jess. It's Patrice. You're listed as Roxy's only contact. I'm sorry to tell you this, but she's had a stroke.'

'Oh. How bad is it?'

'Pretty bad. I should've asked you earlier, but does Roxy have a DNR? A living will? Do you know?'

'Give me a sec.' I put the phone on the desk and take a deep breath. I should feel something – sadness, shock, concern – but I don't.

I open the bottom drawer and flip through the tabs. I'm looking for Roxy's name, but I'm pretty sure I don't have any paperwork from her. I'm right, there's nothing – no will, no contact number, no attorney's name, certainly not a DNR.

'I've got no file on her,' I tell Patrice. 'She might have something in her booth or at her house.'

'Would it be too much trouble to see if you can locate a directive? It's the kind of thing we like to have on hand in a situation like this.'

'I'll have a look. You'll keep me posted?'

'Sure.'

I say good-bye, and then, without paying any attention to the route, make my way to Roxy's booth.

The cabinets and drawers are full of instruments. Large instruments – saxophones, violins, and trombones – are stored in the roomy cubbies; I haul the cases out, open them, pat the linings. Then I duck deep into the cubbies

< 197 >

and run my fingers over the surfaces, thinking that maybe she taped an envelope somewhere. She was secretive and sly. It's just the kind of thing she would do.

On to the drawers, same drill. I grab the cases of flutes and clarinets, open them, inspect the interiors. I pluck them from their beds and peer into the tubing. Then I yank the drawers from their rails, examining the backs and bottoms.

'What're you doing?' Lizzie's voice brings me back to my surroundings. She gazes curiously at me from beyond the front counter, scanning the area.

Disassembled instruments are strewn all around me – trombone bells, trumpet bodies, clarinet and oboe mouthpieces, violin bows and saxophone necks. The cabinet doors are flung open and the large drawers rest upside down. I've made a huge mess. I've been unaware, completely and frantically out of control.

'I've told them again and again – leave instructions.' My voice is tight with near-hysteria. 'I've been going on about it for months. Tell me what you want me to do, I've begged them. If you don't tell me, tell someone. And now Roxy's had a stroke and all they want is some paperwork, which is reasonable. People need to know what to do. But there's no documentation of any kind. There never is.'

I'm almost in tears and I don't know why. Lizzie looks at me like I'm demented. Entering the booth, taking care not to knock her injured leg, she carefully picks her way through the instrument wreckage and sinks to a cross-legged position. Her knee grazes mine.

'These old people around here are just crazy, and that's all there is to it.'

'Yeah.' I sniff.

'Your phone's ringing.' She stretches her arm up to the counter, retrieves the phone, and hands it to me.

< 198 >

'Hello?'

'Jess? It's Patrice. I'm sorry to tell you, your friend just passed away.'

'Oh. Okay. Thanks for letting me know, Patrice.' I turn the phone off and sit there for a few seconds, feeling like part of the disarray that's scattered around us. 'Roxy died. She left absolutely nothing telling me what she wants done with all these instruments.'

'You could donate them.'

'Right.' Like the vendors would allow that. 'You're going to have to give the figurine back to Sue.'

'Which one?'

'You took more than one?'

'A bird and a squirrel.'

'The bird.'

'Are you mad at me?'

'No.'

'Why not?'

'I don't have the energy.'

'Did your mom leave you this place when she died?'

'Yeah.' I sigh, thinking how I didn't just inherit the business; I inherited all the troublesome old people that came with it.

'What was she like?'

'She was just an ordinary person. She didn't like a lot of drama and she always did what needed to be done. A lot like me, actually.'

'Where's your father?'

'Huh. In Oregon, last I heard.'

'Do you ever see him?'

'Never met the man.'

'Do you think I look like Daddy?'

'Yes.'

< 199 >

'Mom said Daddy had strong genes. She said I had his eyes. And she said Christy and Cassie did, too.'

I cringe when she brings up my little girls. I shift so that our knees are no longer touching. Sensing that she's gone too far, she changes the subject.

'Am I ever going to get to ride a horse?'

'We'll see.' I know better than to make a promise. There's a place that used to take horseback tours into Palo Duro Canyon. I'll look into it.

'I bet you were a good teacher.'

'I was.'

'Did you like it?'

'Yes.'

'Why did you stop?'

'I didn't want to do it anymore.'

Why would I do something I enjoyed when my babies are gone? Why would I get up every morning and go to a school and teach children when my children are no more?

'Did you want to do this?' Her tone is disparaging as she gestures toward the mess I've made. All these instruments. Dammit, Roxy.

'Do you think you'll keep playing your flute when school starts?'

'I might. I haven't decided if it's my passion.'

'Passion. Huh. We've got to get your nose out of those romance paperbacks.'

< 200 >

Freezer Stash

I offer Lizzie ten bucks to put Roxy's booth back in order. When she returns to the office an hour later, she's got a tiny case in her hand.

'You took a piccolo?' I ask. She's a larcenous child.

'Flute players often also play the piccolo.' I suspect she's quoting the new teacher, whom I haven't met yet.

'Don't let any of the vendors know.'

They'd expect me to buy that piccolo and divide the payment between all of them. When it comes to money, the vendors are cagey, obsessed, and suspicious; and Roxy was as miserly and paranoid as any of them. I bet she kept a stash somewhere. She's got no box in the safe, and there's nothing secreted away in her booth.

'I'm going out to Roxy's to poke around,' I tell Lizzie. 'You want to come?'

'Sure.'

Because Roxy left her house abruptly last night, it's open today – front and back doors gaping, lights on. Even with the overnight breeze having swept through, her house reeks of tobacco. Inside, I struggle to raise the windows in their grime-encrusted railings, managing to get several inches of air. I prop the doors even wider in the hope that fresh air might make the odor bearable. With Lizzie flanking me, I do a cursory walk-through as I try to work my way into

< 201 >

the mind-set of a mean-spirited shifty old woman. Where would she hide her money? I've come to the back room, the storage area full of broken and useless items. I'll start here and work my way forward.

'What are we looking for?' Lizzie asks. 'Can I keep stuff?'

'What kind of stuff?'

'You know, just stuff we need.' What could she be talking about? We don't need anything.

'Okay.'

She heads back toward the living room, eager to forage.

Nothing in this room has changed. The clutter disturbs me. Shapeless pillows, beat-up lampshades, thin towels, scarred furniture, broken appliances, the chair-with-hair-dryer – where's the value in any of it?

I lift, dig, open, shift, and climb. Lizzie interrupts me once, asking for the car key. It takes nearly an hour to search the room. I trip and almost fall twice as I try to navigate the dense jumble. Before I move to Roxy's bedroom, I go in search of Lizzie. She's out at the car, loading the trunk and back seat with bits of Roxy's life. She's taken several things she knows we don't need – throw pillows, doilies, a mantel clock, a set of coasters. And she's taken a couple of things she thinks we need – a lamp and a microwave. It all stinks of cigarette smoke.

'How'd you get that microwave out here?'

'I carried it.' She's stronger than she looks.

'I guess your hands are feeling better.'

I go back inside and continue poking around in Roxy's room. A while later Lizzie hollers at me, excitement in her voice. I rush out the door and down the hallway.

'Look at this.' She stands in the middle of the living room. One of the chairs has been pushed back, a square portion of carpet has been removed, and, while the rest

< 202 >

of the floor is concrete, the newly bared section reveals a wooden cover, two feet by two feet. 'A hidden compartment. Is this what we're looking for?'

'Could be. How'd you find it?'

'The carpet was wrinkled funny around the chair.'

'Open it and let's have a look.'

'I'm not going to open it. You open it.'

I squat and, working my fingers between the concrete and splintery wood, lift the cover.

Etch-a-sketches, nothing else. About twenty-five of them. Red plastic casing, gray-white screens, little white knobs. Flabbergasted, I fall back from squatting position to sitting cross-legged. This is what she stored in her super-secret specially constructed hiding place?

'Hey, I need one of these.' Pleased, Lizzie reaches in and grabs one.

'Sometimes I'm just too amazed for words.'

Leaving her sitting there fiddling with the Etch-a-sketch, I return to Roxy's bedroom. I've been through all of her drawers, her closet, and her nightstand. I even checked beneath the bed and between the mattress and box spring. Taking a cue from Lizzie, I shift the furniture around a bit, thinking maybe I'll find another concealed storage area. But there's nothing.

I duck into the bathroom and give it a thorough going-over, lifting the lid of the toilet tank, shifting through lotions and cotton balls on the shelves in the cabinet, groping beneath towels and washcloths. There's nothing unusual.

It's a small house. Only two rooms left – the living room, which Lizzie's already gone through, and the kitchen. I head to the kitchen.

Roxy's purse hangs by its strap on the back of a chair. I go

< 203 >

through it, extracting her wallet, which contains two crisp hundred-dollar bills. I take them out, fold them, and stuff them in the front pocket of my baggy shorts. I check her driver's license. It expired last year. Born November twentieth, 1933. I find prescription bottles in a three-drawer column. All colors, all sizes, all empty. Hundreds of them, labels dating back to the seventies.

One of the lower cabinets is full of plastic containers, the kind that come free with lunchmeat. I estimate seventy. Lids are stacked separately.

Further down below the counter, another three drawers overflow with coupons. Torn from newspapers and magazines. Roxy wasn't the type to cut when she could rip. I pluck one out and scan it. Bounty paper towels. Buy one, get one free. Expired five years ago.

'Jessica, I'm getting bored.' Leaning in the doorway, she lifts her shirt and examines her scabby midsection. The abrasions look red and sore. She scratches at one of the scabs.

'Don't pick at it,' I tell her. 'One more quick look and we're out of here.'

I open the refrigerator. Nothing of interest, not even much food – mostly condiments like mustard, ketchup, mayonnaise, barbecue sauce. I open the freezer and find what I'm looking for. Frozen inside a huge block of ice is a dark cube. I'm pretty sure it's a small reinforced safe, the type that's found in hotel closets and advertised for home use on infomercials. I reach in, grab it, and, working it out over the rough ice of a freezer that badly needs defrosting, set it on the counter.

'Is that what we're looking for?' Lizzie asks.

'I think so, yeah.'

< 204 >

My fingers are stinging from the frozen cold. Grabbing a dishtowel from its hook, I adjust the fabric so that it protects the palms of both my hands. Then I carry the frozen cube through the house and out the front door. The chunk is starting to grow slippery as I dump it into the open trunk.

Roxy's stuff makes the interior of my car smell like Roxy's house. I roll down the windows and the wind sweeps through so that our hair whips at our faces all the way home.

< 205 >

Clueless Joe

I wake up at five a.m. Lizzie's still asleep. Last night I dumped the frozen chunk from Roxy's into the sink. This morning the ice has fully melted to reveal what I expected. The combination is Roxy's birthday. The safe holds about seventy thousand in cash – nice and dry because the door's sealed. I immediately transfer the funds to my larger safe. I do all this shifting around with sneaky steps and furtive movements because I don't want Lizzie to wake up and witness my sly theft – but honestly, theft from whom? A dead woman? Does that really count as theft? I dry the outside of the safe and leave it sitting on the counter, next to the newly acquired microwave.

When Lizzie gets up and sees the safe open and empty, she asks what was in it.

'Nothing,' I say. 'It's just like her to keep something like that and never use it.'

She looks dubious.

'You can have it.'

'Really?' Pleased, she wraps her arms around the substantial box, lugs it to her corner, drops it on the bed, and says, 'I've been needing one of these.'

Later, when I go downstairs, I'm told that there's going to be a meeting at ten o'clock in Pard's double-sized booth. It takes Ken and Barry, working together, three times longer

< 206 >

than it took me, working alone, to set up the chairs for the last meeting.

The atmosphere on the second floor is tense. As anticipated, the vendors are feeling mutinous about Dee's booth going to the highest bidder. Also, they're anxious about what's going to happen to the contents of Roxy's booth. Though it's been promised that I'll have a chance to have my say, I bet mainly what I'll end up doing is listening to them tell me how I'm doing everything wrong and how they won't tolerate any shady dealings when it comes to Roxy's instruments. I take my place on the front row. Sherman steps front and center, gives a brief greeting, and gets started.

'Location has always been based on seniority.' He shakes a finger at me, glaring from behind his thick lenses. 'You got no right to change that.'

'Well, Sherman, you've been here longer than anybody, except maybe Abe. Do you want Dee's booth?'

He hasn't repositioned an item in his area for as long as I've known him. If he can't be stirred to move a couple of WWI helmets from one shelf to the other, I can't see him wanting to haul his entire inventory downstairs.

'That's not the point.'

'Then what is?'

'That this isn't about money. It's about doing things the right way. I may not want the booth, but I should be offered it. I got first dibs.'

Lizzie flies in, flutters around, and alights in the empty chair on the second row next to Sylvia, who's still in disgrace over the typewriters. Lizzie's wearing the same shorts and T-shirt she wore yesterday, so it's time for another trip to the laundromat. Or maybe she needs more clothes – she only brought one suitcase, and it wasn't large.

< 207 >

'Your mother never would have … blah, blah, blah.'

I stop listening when he brings my mother into it. For the whole time she owned this place Mom charged exactly the same for each booth, whether it was on the second floor rear or first floor front-and-center. That was her call and this is mine. Dee's second-from-the-door booth gets more traffic, so whoever has it should pay more. Sherman can talk until he dies, but I'm going to do it my way and there's not a thing he can do about it. When I start listening again, they've moved on.

'I guess we should just split up her inventory,' Kathryn says.

'Or one of us could take all of it and buy everybody out.' This from Barry.

I roll my eyes. The elderlies are sparkling with the enthusiasm that accompanies an original and brilliant plan. Like this hasn't been said before. Like this isn't the exact same conversation that took place the last time one of them died.

'You know what would've been helpful?' I'm compelled to say it again. 'If Roxy had left some sort of instruction about what she wanted done. Like whether she wanted to be cremated or buried, or who she wanted to give her instruments to, or her car or even her house. If any of you have such a document, or get one drawn up, I'll gladly keep it on file in my office.'

'You're like a broken record,' Genevieve says.

'We're sick of hearing about it,' Will says.

Lizzie distracts us all by waving her arms high over her head. Everyone looks at her.

'Have you thought about donating the instruments?' she asks. 'The music program in my school back in Dayton is always broke, so I guess it's probably the same here.'

Her suggestion is met with a collective gasp, then

< 208 >

appalled silence. Sylvia scoots over a chair, creating distance between herself and the little traitor. Lizzie, seeing the reaction, looks at me with a question in her eyes. Oh, Grasshopper.

Without another word, heads shaking in sad disapproval, the group disbands.

I wander down to the basement. When it came to making a decision about whether or not to claim Roxy's ashes, I decided to keep her. She taught me a lesson about what not to become. I saw an urn in Audrey's booth that was the exact same shade as Roxy's hair.

'You looking for something for Roxy?' Audrey asks, coming up behind me.

'How about that one?' I point to the pearly pink container.

'I love that one. It's so pretty.' It's nice but kind of creepy that she's so fond of her merchandise. 'Just a heads-up – they're saying upstairs how you need to divide Roxy's portion of the gun money and distribute it.'

I pull my phone from my pocket and divide Roxy's portion – thirty-two dollars – by the number of vendors. It comes to seventy cents. They can accuse and complain all they want, but I'll be damned if I'm going to walk through the building distributing two quarters and two dimes to each vendor.

'How much for the urn?' I ask.

'A hundred and twenty.'

'I bet I can find it new for a hundred on the internet.'

'Whatever you think's best.' She shuffles behind the counter and sinks into her chair.

'You're going to fit right in here,' I tell her, heading back upstairs to order an urn that's never been used before and is reasonably priced.

< 209 >

Joe's waiting outside my office with Lizzie. He looks uninterested as she tells him about the progress of her injuries – and the scowl of boredom that weighs upon his features makes me realize that, for all his lecturing about how I should handle Lizzie, he probably isn't a very good father to his children. In fact, his indifference looks a lot like Don's when he had to endure a conversation that wasn't about him.

'The bottom of my feet got better by the next day,' she says, 'but I still can't get my stitches wet, so I haven't had a full bath or shower in days. I think I'll be able to ride my bike tomorrow.'

'Hey, Joe. You could have come in and had a seat.' I move past him, enter the office, circle the desk, and sit. 'Lizzie, you need to go upstairs and clean your area. Gather your clothes. Laundry this afternoon.'

'But I wanted to show Joe my new phone.'

'Joe's seen phones before. Go on. I mean it.'

She stamps her foot in feeble protest, then tromps out the door.

'Cracking the whip,' Joe says as he follows me in and takes the chair. 'I like it.'

'What can I do for you?'

'I'm sorry about your friend.'

'Yeah. We're all kind of in shock.'

'The Arckles'll be charged with murder.'

'Well, that's justice, I suppose. But it's not going to make a difference to Roxy.'

'Except for that one email, Humboldt's daughter hasn't heard back from him.'

'I thought he was in Dallas.'

'Yeah, that's the story. It's just, this is the last place he was seen. You know his daughter's got a sick kid?'

< 210 >

'How would I know that?'

'The Arckles are saying Roxy told them you had the cards in your safe.' He gives a nod toward the safe. 'Do you have any baseball cards?' Does he want me to invite him to see for himself? That's not going to happen.

'We've been over this and the answer's still no. Roxy brought those thugs here because it's all she could think to do. When people are scared and in trouble around here, I'm the one they turn to.'

'So I went out to her house, just to have a look around.'

My heart rate picks up and my stomach clenches, but I know how to maintain a semblance of calm when what I want to do is scream. He'll never know I'm panicking inside.

'Did you find anything?'

'I've never seen so much old and useless stuff. No baseball cards. No firearms. Nothing out there that has anything to do with anything. She had one of those chairs with a plastic hood that comes down, for drying hair, like they have in beauty shops. Why would someone have one of those in their house? And old sheets and towels, everything stinking of cigarette smoke. Didn't she throw anything away?'

'Beats me.'

'So, this is what I know. Raymond Verney comes to town. He asks his ex-wife for the baseball cards that he left with her years ago. She's glad to give them to him because she's got so much junk, she's thrilled to get something out of the house.' For his whole life Joe will only see things in the context of his own point of view. 'Then she forgets she even saw him because her brain doesn't work anymore. So he puts them in the trunk of his car, then meets up with his friend, Arthur Humboldt, who's traveling from Oklahoma back to Vegas. But instead of going home, where

< 211 >

his daughter and a sick kid are waiting, they go to Dallas to visit a friend, no name, and nobody's heard from them since.'

'If it's what happened, then it's what happened.'

'Yeah, even if it's not the way I would have done things. But people do things that don't make sense all the time, right?' He's quoting my own line back to me. 'I sent a description of both their cars to Dallas. They'll turn up there eventually.' He stands and with a 'See you later' walks out the door.

That afternoon, rather than taking Lizzie to do laundry, I take her to Penney's to buy some shorts and tops. Instead of being excited that I'm buying her new clothes, she complains about how the only place I ever shop is Penney's. When we get home, her new Kindle has arrived. She's thrilled to have it. When she realizes it's pre-loaded with her reading list, she laughs at me.

'You're such a schoolteacher,' she says. 'And what are these two other books? They're not on the list.'

'They're on Caprock's list.'

'Why would I care what they're reading in Caprock?'

'They're good books that everybody should read.'

'Mom'll be back to get me when she said she'd be.'

'Nobody's saying differently.'

'Then why did you get me Caprock's reading list?'

'I told you – they're good books.'

'Mom'll be back.'

'Hmm.'

Maybe, maybe not. We'll see.

< 212 >

Acknowledgements

People like to know where I get my ideas. *Why Stuff Matters* was inspired by Market Place Antiques and Collectibles on I-10 in Houston, which is a huge building populated by elderly vendors who overprice their stuff. Add that to the fact that I've lived in seven different countries in thirty years; well, I learned how easy it is to get rid of stuff, get new stuff, and then get rid of that, too. It's just stuff.

I'd like to acknowledge the Singapore American Women's Association's Writers' Group, a supportive circle of friends who listened and advised, and put up with the way I read so fast with my Texas accent. Special thanks to Teresa Zink, who introduced me to my agent: in a business that's often competitive and stingy with contacts, Teresa is generous when it comes to making introductions and helping other writers meet their goals.

I recognize and recommend the MFA program of Fairleigh-Dickinson, which nurtured my ability, process, confidence, and passion for writing – especially Ellen Akins, who is a gifted writer, reviewer, and editor.

Also, thanks to my agent, Helen Mangham, of the Jacaranda Literary Agency, who is dedicated to writers and literature; and the people at Arcadia – Joe Harper, Piers Russell-Cobb, and my editors, Luke Brown and Angeline Rothermundt, who were supportive, enthusiastic, and committed to making this project flawless.